"You're staring."

Spence pulled out his best grin. "I was just thinking that before you leave I should print out a picture of what poison ivy looks like. You know, just in case you happen to see it again."

Deena stiffened slightly. "I may be rusty on classifying plants, but I don't need a photograph." Back straight, she marched from the room in a huff.

When he'd insisted that Alyssa attend this camp, he'd been picturing someone else entirely in the role of cabin counselor. In his mind's eye, he'd pictured a woman with the godliness of Mother Teresa and the maternal skills of June Cleaver.

Instead, he'd gotten Wonder Woman meets Madame Curie. He struggled to conceal a wave of disappointment. Just what was God thinking, sending a scientist into Alyssa's life?

KIM O'BRIEN grew up in Bronxville, New York, with her family and many pets—fish, cats, dogs, gerbils, guinea pigs, parakeets, and even a big thoroughbred horse named Pops. She worked for many years as a writer, editor, and speechwriter for IBM in New York. She holds a Master of Fine Arts in Writing from Sarah Lawrence College in Bronxville, New York, and is active in the Fellowship of The Woodlands Church. She lives in The Woodlands, Texas, with her husband, two daughters, and, of course, pets.

Books by Kim O' Brien

HEARTSONG PRESENTS
HP641—The Pastor's Assignment

Leap
of Faith

Kim O'Brien

Heartsong Presents

Special thanks to Jenny Chang, MD, for answering my questions and generously allowing me to visit her laboratory at the Baylor School of Medicine, and to Melissa Landis, PhD, who gave me my first view of a cancer cell. These are extraordinary women doing extraordinary work. Any factual errors in the book relating to breast cancer are mine.

A note from the Author:
I love to hear from my readers! You may correspond with me by writing:

Kim O'Brien
Author Relations
PO Box 721
Uhrichsville, OH 44683

ISBN 978-1-60260-263-2

LEAP OF FAITH

All scripture quotations are taken from the HOLY BIBLE, NEW INTERNATIONAL VERSION®. NIV®. Copyright © 1973, 1978, 1984 by International Bible Society. Used by permission of Zondervan. All rights reserved.

All of the characters and events in this book are fictitious. Any resemblance to actual persons, living or dead, or to actual events is purely coincidental.

Our mission is to publish and distribute inspirational products offering exceptional value and biblical encouragement to the masses.

PRINTED IN THE U.S.A.

one

"Stacy, what in the world do you think you're doing?" Dr. Deena Bradley stared down at her sister—seven months pregnant, plopped on top of a bulging suitcase. The lid had caved in under Stacy, and clothing protruded from the gaping sides.

"Packing." Stacy tugged impatiently at the zipper. "Or trying to, but it won't shut. Packing these maternity clothes is like packing parachutes."

Deena reached out her hand to pull her sister from the suitcase. "The only place you're going is to bed. Remember what the doctor said."

"Get away." Stacy slapped Deena's hands away, and her pointed chin lifted a notch. "Evie's camp starts in three days."

Blue eyes met blue eyes. When her sister's chin came up like this, Deena knew she was sunk. While Deena had two years and almost six inches over her, Stacy had inherited the genes for stubbornness.

Deena put her hands on her hips. There had to be a few genes for stubbornness in her DNA chain. And even if there weren't, she knew the one sure way to get Stacy back in bed. "Don't make me call Jeff."

Stacy's features changed abruptly at the mention of her husband's name. "Oh, Deena. You can't do that. Please don't ask him to come home from work early. He thinks his poetry is soothing, but it's driving me crazy. One more ode to our unborn child and I'm burning his rhyming dictionary."

Deena hid a smile. Jeff had a great heart but wrote terrible poetry. His last work, read at Thanksgiving, dealt with grief over a man's inability to become pregnant. "I won't call him, but you've got to get back in bed." She closed her fingers around

Stacy's petite wrists and leaned backward, helping her up from the suitcase.

Tucking Stacy into the king-size bed, Deena perched on the edge. "You know, bed rest isn't the end of the world."

Stacy stared at her as if she were crazy. "I can't just lie here for eight weeks."

"Yes, you can. School's out, remember?"

"Yeah, but I'm snack mom for Jack's soccer camp. And I'm chaperoning five girls at Camp Bald Eagle, remember?"

"I'll buy snacks for Jack's team, and you can send Evie to camp without you."

"Send Evie alone?" Stacy shook her head. "No way. She'll just get into trouble."

"So keep her home, then."

"Not an option." Stacy's chin came up. "She needs this camp."

"So send her, then. How much trouble can a kid get into at a church camp?"

Stacy just lifted her brows.

"She's twelve. You have to let go sometime."

"And sometimes you've got to know when to hold on." Stacy pleated the fabric of the embroidered ivory bedspread. "She's got the hormone thing starting. One minute she's happy, the next in tears. Everything I say to her is wrong, and then she just wants to cuddle."

She pushed the covers back, but Deena pulled them up just as firmly. "Stacy, stop it."

"I appreciate you coming and all." Stacy pushed the covers off again. "But I know how busy you are with your lab and your experiments. There are some snickerdoodles on the counter. You ought to take some when you go."

"I'm not going anywhere." Not that she hadn't had one eye on the clock. "And neither are you."

"If I back out now, the church is going to have a hard time finding someone to replace me."

Deena stared at the hollows under her sister's eyes, the

paleness of her skin, the fingers so swollen from pregnancy that she couldn't even wear her wedding ring. "They'll find someone. It isn't something for you to worry about."

"I'm her mother, Deena. It's my job to worry."

The unspoken "If you had children, you would understand" hung in the air between them. Just as it had when Stacy had dropped out of graduate school just credits shy of her master's degree in physics. And before that when Stacy had traded her fitness club membership so her son could play on a fancy sports team.

Rising, Deena crossed the room to pull back the lace curtain. Like everything else in the house, it was old but lovingly cared for.

She peered into the backyard. No, she didn't understand how someone could love others so much and always put herself last. But then again, Stacy could never seem to accept Deena's choices either. "You bury yourself in work," Stacy always accused. "You have no life."

A stockade fence in which no two posts stood the same height surrounded a yard desperately in need of a good mowing. Jeff had built the fence, just as he had Jack's tree house, which Deena always referred to as the Leaning Tower of Pizza. That thing just couldn't be safe.

Her world was completely different. Instead of tree houses, backyard baseball games, and kids, Deena had her laboratory at the University of Connecticut Health Center. Her cell culture room might not seem very cozy to other people, but Deena loved the small room with an incubator keeping tissue samples cold and the sterile work area behind a plate glass hood. She felt at home among the glass pipettes and trays of subculture plates. Deena might not be good at reading bedtime stories, but she was very good at reading the story the cell samples told her as she studied them beneath her inverted microscope.

Jack walked into the backyard along with Godzilla, their harlequin Great Dane. Where was Evie? Deena wouldn't have put it past the girl to be planning another prank. The other night Stacy had called her in despair because Evie had gotten on the intercom at the local supermarket and announced a half-price doughnut sale at the bakery. "What am I going to do with her?" Stacy had said.

The pranks were harmless but seemed to be escalating. Stacy wouldn't send Evie alone to camp, and if Evie stayed home, she'd make it impossible for Stacy to rest. There was only one solution.

Deena let the curtain fall back into place. "I'll go, Stace. I'll take your place at the camp."

Stacy laughed. "You're kidding, right?"

"No."

"You're brilliant, Deena, and you'll probably cure breast cancer someday. But when it comes to kids. . ." Stacy shook her head sadly. "Let's just say you aren't Mary Poppins."

Deena lifted her eyebrows. "I may not have children, but I have Mr. Crackers. I understand regular care and feeding."

"These are kids, not a parrot. You'd have a nervous break-down within three days. You have to build up your endurance before you can be around kids full-time."

"I made it through Christmas and Easter, remember?"

"Holidays are different. Besides, this is a Christian camp."

"I'm a Christian."

"You need to be able to model your faith, Deena, pray with the kids, and help them understand how much God loves them."

"I can do that." Deena lifted a photograph off the top of the mahogany dresser. The picture was an old one now, taken when her mother was still in good health. Before the breast cancer.

In the picture her mother was the exact age Deena was now, and the similarities were striking. They had the same arched black eyebrows, fair skin, and light blue eyes. Their smiles matched, as did the single freckle on the left side of Deena's mouth. The only difference was their hairstyle. Evelyn had worn hers in a wavy, shoulder-length shag; Deena preferred a modified pixie cut.

"I have to drag you to church," Stacy pointed out.

"I have a very busy schedule," Deena hedged. "Mine isn't a nine-to-five kind of job."

Stacy pulled herself higher against the pillows. "Exactly. You haven't taken a vacation in years. Are you telling me that you would take a week off?"

What would her mother have looked like now? Deena set the photograph back on the dresser. She'd have to clear it with Dr. Chin, but she thought Olson and Papish, both highly trained researchers, could fill in for her. "Yes. I'll take my laptop and keep tabs from the jungle."

"Not a jungle, Deena. Northwestern Connecticut. The foot-hills of the Berkshires."

"You know what I mean." Deena swallowed. "So what do you think?"

"I don't think you can do it."

Deena feared her sister might be right, but she was more afraid of losing her sister than failing as a camp counselor. "Stacy, I'll take good care of Evie. I promise."

Stacy's face turned very red, just as it always did when she was about to cry. Her sister had inherited not only the stubborn genes but also the emotional ones. Her nose turned red at the tip. Her lips trembled, but her eyes held a mixture of relief and gratitude. "Are you sure?"

Deena looked around for the box of tissues. "Yeah, Stacy, I'm sure."

Stacy sighed. "I know Evie can't stay here, and I can't go to camp. So thank you, Deena. I'll call Pastor Rich first thing in the morning."

two

Deena was bent over unpacking her suitcase when she felt a thump on her shoulder. Screaming, she spun around, ready to battle whatever monster had jumped onto her inside this awful, musty-smelling cabin. It was only Evie, though, who stood behind her, grinning broadly. The other girls were laughing, too.

"Got you, Aunt Deena," Evie said. "Got you good."

"That you did." Deena struggled to take the prank with good humor. Her nerves still jangled from that two-hour bus ride. All that screaming—and if she heard one more rendition of "Ninety-nine Bottles of Root Beer on the Wall," she'd have to be institutionalized. What had she gotten herself into?

She forced a smile. "I thought a bat landed on my shoulder."

"Bats are nocturnal," a small girl with Clark Kent glasses and honey-colored hair said. Her camp T-shirt, the same one Deena and the others wore, looked about six sizes too big for her.

"Yes, they are," Deena agreed. "Unless they're rabid."

This of course turned out to be the completely wrong thing to say because it immediately caused all the girls to flutter around in girlish horror, requiring Deena to assure them the possibility of a rabid bat flying into their cabin was practically nonexistent.

"Well, if one came in," said a pretty blond-haired girl wearing way too much makeup, "I'd, like, spray it with my Freeze and Shine."

"You can't kill a bat with hairspray." A red-haired girl, also wearing heavy eye makeup, punctuated her sentence with a huge pink bubble. Deena watched in fascination as it grew to the size of the girl's head before shriveling and then disappearing back into her mouth.

"Maybe not kill it," the blond agreed, "but it'd stun it for sure. Spray enough of it and Freeze and Shine could, like, plaster that bat to the cabin wall."

Deena sat down on the bed. This wasn't going as she'd expected. Not at all. Somehow she'd pictured the kids more like her grad students, respectful of her professorial status and eager to learn from her. She'd pictured herself showing them the constellations at night, not debating the holding power of Freeze and Shine hairspray. She deliberately pushed Stacy's voice to the back of her mind. Stacy didn't think she would last three days. Deena would make the full week even if it killed her.

And it very well might. The cabin smelled musty and wasn't air-conditioned. The bunk beds had mattresses that felt like they'd been stuffed with straw, and she hadn't seen a single power outlet for her laptop.

"Hey." A dark-skinned, heavyset girl with gorgeous curly black hair peered down at the cage at Deena's feet. "Is that a bird?"

The girl tried to peek beneath the cloth covering, but Deena moved the cage protectively closer. "He's an African Grey. A parrot," she clarified. Stacy had been very specific that she needed to speak like a person and not a scientist.

"What's his name? Can I see him? Does he bite?" The questions came faster and louder, overlapping. It seemed the girls didn't want answers as much as they wanted to be the one voice that would be heard above all others.

Before she could stop it, someone lifted the cloth covering. A big "ooh" went up as Mr. Crackers flexed his back.

"Hello," the dark-haired girl said. "Polly want a cracker?"

Mr. Crackers looked terrified. He said, "Shake your groove thing."

Music was one of Deena's guilty pleasures, especially pop rock, and the bird had picked up a lot of lyrics as a result. She jerked the cloth back in place. "Let the bird rest, okay? You can see him later."

She could have left the bird home with one of her grad

students, but Deena hadn't been able to bring herself to do so. Having adopted Mr. Crackers from a former colleague, she suspected the parrot had abandonment issues complicated by low self-esteem.

She ran her fingers through her hair. *Think, Deena. This is just like when you were a graduate student and Dr. English handed you that stack of data and asked you to make sense of it. And it was an impossible mess until you sorted it out, broke it down into categories, and organized it.* Possibly the same technique could be used with kids. First she would gather data.

Deena pulled out her clipboard. Just holding it in her hands made her feel more like herself. "Okay," she said loudly, drowning out the voices eagerly swapping information about what pets had been left at home. "I'm going to take roll call. Please tell me a bit about yourself." She looked at the first name. "Alyssa Rossi?"

The small, honey-colored-haired girl raised her arm. "Here."

"You want to tell me something about yourself?"

Alyssa dug into her shorts pocket and pulled out a folded piece of paper. "My uncle said to give you this."

The list was a duplicate of the one Deena had in Alyssa's file. Prior to coming to the camp, Deena had been given information about each of the girls. Alyssa was the allergy girl—dust, mites, pollen, mold, pine, pet dander, bees, grass. . . . The girl also had moderate asthma, mostly triggered by pollution, anxiety, or intense physical activity. Deena was supposed to carry a rescue inhaler and EpiPen on her at all times.

"Anything else? Special interests?"

The girl shook her head. "None."

"Okay, then," Deena said. "Evie Matthews?"

"Present and accounted for." Evie saluted her.

"What do you like to do for fun?" Deena tried a more specific question this time.

"Play video games and listen to my Zune."

"Oh, what tunes?" Deena asked, genuinely enjoying the opportunity to get to know her niece better.

"Not tunes," Evie corrected. "Zune. It's sort of like an iPod, but Microsoft makes it and you can download videos and squirt music."

Deena had no idea what squirting music meant. In fact, it sounded kind of gross. She didn't want to look stupid by asking more, so she turned to the next name on her list. "Thank you, Evie. Now, who's Lourdes Sanchez?"

The heavyset girl with the gorgeous black hair raised her hand. "That's me." The minute she opened her mouth, Deena spied a full set of braces complete with purple and red rubber bands crisscrossing in an elaborate pattern. "I play the guitar and like writing. My dad is the music minister at our church."

"What kind of writing?" Deena prompted, thinking she might be on more familiar ground here.

"I blog, mostly."

"Are you on, like, MySpace or Facebook?" asked the pretty blond who had brought the Freeze and Shine hairspray.

"MySpace," Lourdes informed her.

"You're Britty, right?" Deena smiled encouragingly at the blond. "Britty Trekland?"

"Yeah. I like hanging out with my friends." Here she paused to grin at the red-haired girl next to her. "Taylor and I are cousins."

Taylor Anderson, the redhead, also wore a copious amount of makeup and chewed vigorously on a wad of gum. "Britty's parents and mine are going on vacation to Switzerland for a week, so they sent us here. They said it was a good deal."

"Well," Deena said bravely, "I'm sure we're all going to become good friends."

There was general agreement, and Taylor sealed the deal by unveiling half a suitcase full of candy. Each girl took a piece of chocolate, except for Allergy Girl, who reluctantly settled on a Life Saver after carefully reading the ingredients list. The girls held up their candy as if they were making a toast. "To friends," Taylor said. The others echoed her and popped the candy into their mouths.

"Okay, then," Deena said. "What's next?"

Evie was already in motion. "Explore. We want to explore the camp!"

❧

Hours later Deena turned off the cabin lights and climbed into the top bunk. The mattress, lumpy as it was, felt like heaven as she settled herself beneath the cool sheets.

Below her Alyssa stirred, gently shaking the boards of the wooden bunk. No problem—an earthquake couldn't have kept Deena awake. She put her hand under her pillow in her sleeping position.

She smiled. It had been a good day. They'd seen the archery fields, the pool, and the stables. They'd wanted to see the boys' cabins, but she'd talked them into a nature walk instead. The hike had been hugely successful. They'd watched a family of white-tailed deer bound through the woods, picked flowers in a field full of daisies, and pretended a fallen log was a balance beam and practiced leaping dismounts. After dinner, Pastor Rich had led an upbeat praise and worship time that had included a guest appearance by a Christian magician.

"Miss Deena?"

She opened one eye, listened, and then closed it again. Just that one little motion seemed to take all the energy she had.

"Miss Deena?" the voice whispered in the darkness.

Good grief. It was past midnight. Where did anyone get the energy? Deena rolled to the edge of the bunk and peered over the edge. "You okay, Alyssa?"

"I think I need my allergy medication."

"Oh, honey," Deena said sympathetically. The girl was probably homesick. This wasn't particularly surprising. "You took your allergy medicine right after dinner."

"I know." A pause. "But I think I'm having an allergic reaction."

An allergic reaction? Deena opened both eyes. "What are your symptoms?" It was entirely possible there'd been something in those sloppy joe sandwiches. Deena hadn't digested them very well herself.

"I itch." In the darkness Alyssa's voice sounded small and youthful. "My arm is super itchy."

Deena felt for the slats of the bunk ladder with her feet and crawled down the side of the bunk bed. She nearly tripped over a pair of sneakers as she retrieved the flashlight from the night table. "Show me."

The girl, pale and elfin-looking in yet another man-sized T-shirt, held out a thin white arm.

It was red where Alyssa had been scratching, and Deena could just make out a few small red bumps. "I don't think it's an allergic reaction, honey. I think you got bit by a couple of very hungry mosquitoes." She patted the girl's shoulder. "We'll put some Benadryl cream on it and you'll feel much better."

"Maybe I should use my rescue inhaler."

"Are you having trouble breathing?"

The girl shook her head.

"Then let's try the cream first."

As she shuffled her way through the darkness to her first-aid kit, Deena felt her legs begin to itch. And a spot on her arm, too.

The beam of light found her medical supplies. She searched its contents as quietly as she could, all the while trying to ignore the way her skin itched.

Tube of Benadryl in her hand, she journeyed back to Alyssa. Halfway there, another small voice spoke out of the darkness. "Can I have some, too? My legs really itch."

The voice belonged to Lourdes. Deena turned toward her. "You got bitten, too?" Deena had read all the guide books that Stacy had recommended, even spent time at the local sports shop, peppering the salesperson with questions about camping and hiking. She'd thought she was prepared for anything, but evidently she hadn't counted on the mosquitoes here being so aggressive. From now on she'd make them wear the heavy-duty repellent, not the one that had looked chemically safer for everyone.

"Me, too," Evie said. "My legs really itch."

"And me," Taylor called out.

"Count me in," Britty added. "I would have said something sooner, but I didn't want to wake everyone."

Deena turned on the lights. The girls all gathered around her and extended their arms and legs, all dotted with bite marks and red from scratching.

She began dispensing the Benadryl cream and sympathy. It was going to be a long, long night.

three

The small room they'd given him was no bigger than an oversized closet. At six feet four inches, Spencer Rossi was pretty sure he could lie down and span the length of the room.

He wasn't used to working indoors or having an office, and certainly not being called a nurse. None of these really mattered, though. He'd packed up the house, kenneled his dog, and driven a hundred miles with a kid who had barely spoken to him the entire way. Now he prayed God would do the rest.

He put down the MCAT study guide and took a sip of coffee. Six thirty in the morning. Miss Miriam, the retired nurse who had also volunteered to help at the camp, would be in at eight. Until then, he'd enjoy the solitude. Soon the kids would trickle in for their daily medications. The number of kids on everything from antidepressants to allergy medications amazed him. It hadn't been that way when he and Evan were kids.

"Hello? Are you the camp nurse?"

Spencer looked up as a tall woman with spiky black hair walked into his room. His first thought was that Wonder Woman herself had landed in his clinic. She had light blue eyes and skin the color of fresh cream. Her long legs looked capable of running down the fastest villain, and her waist looked about the size of his watchband.

"Yes. Spencer Rossi." He extended his hand. "How can I help you?"

Wonder Woman shook his hand. "I'm Deena Bradley. We've been up all night itching."

For the first time Spence allowed himself to notice the small group of girls peering around the doorway.

"I thought we'd been bitten by something yesterday," Deena said, "but it's getting worse. Benadryl helps, but it doesn't really stop the itching."

"Let me take a look." Spence bent to pull a pair of latex gloves out of a drawer, and when he straightened, he found himself looking into his niece's large green eyes. "Alyssa?"

The girl produced her arm unhappily. "Hi, Uncle Spence."

"Wait a minute," Deena interrupted. "You're her uncle?"

"And guardian," Spence stated, wanting to make it perfectly clear to Wonder Woman that he wasn't just a relative. Alyssa was his child, and whoever failed to take good care of her would answer to him.

As usual, though, he could tell he'd said the wrong thing. Alyssa stepped back from him and would have moved farther away except he was holding her arm.

"It started last night," Deena explained. "You think maybe it's chigger bites? Bedbugs?"

Spencer turned his niece's arm over and examined both sides. "Nope. Poison ivy."

"Poison ivy?"

"Poison ivy—as in that shiny green plant with three leaves and a red stem."

"I know what poison ivy looks like." Deena riffled her hand through her short hair, making it spikier than ever. "I can't believe I missed it."

Deena didn't look like the kind of woman who spent much time outdoors. "Lots of people wander right into it. What we need to do is make sure we wash all the oils off your skin and under your fingernails so you don't spread it to other parts of your body."

"Girls, I am so sorry."

Spence shrugged. As a wilderness paramedic, he'd seen his share of people baffled by nature. Weekend warriors who thought it would be fun to climb Mount Washington and then the weather turned. Or thrill seekers who found out the hard way that the great outdoors wasn't one big theme park.

He examined Alyssa's legs and the backs of her arms. "You have this rash anywhere else, honey?"

"No."

His niece looked even more awful than usual. Extremely pale, she had huge purple shadows under her eyes and a pinched look around her mouth. Small for her age, the camp shirt—which admittedly he'd ordered in the wrong size—all but swallowed her small frame.

Spence reached for the Tecnu gel and tried to hold his worries in check. With all Alyssa's allergies, she might get a really bad case of poison ivy and need steroids, possibly a trip to the emergency room. He'd hoped this camp would bring them closer together, not add another brick in the wall.

"So where'd you run into the ivy?" Spence rubbed some Tecnu gel on an arm so thin it all but disappeared in his hand.

"In the woods." This came not from Alyssa or the woman, but from a tall girl with copper-colored hair. "We saw deer and found a cool meadow."

Spence frowned. "Did you check yourselves for ticks? I know it seems like it's fun to explore the woods." Here he paused to give Deena a significant look. "But if you don't know what you're doing, you should stay on the path."

Deena's cheeks reddened, and her lips pressed more tightly together. Good. She got the message.

He led his niece to the tiny sink. He washed her arm, dried it, and then smoothed calamine lotion over the area. She let him take care of her, but it was as if they were nothing more than doctor and patient. He wondered if it would always be like that.

He finished with Alyssa and started to work on the next girl, a pretty blond with a high ponytail and a lot of eye makeup. She had a good-sized patch of poison ivy on both her legs, which she probably got, she said cheerfully, when they'd found a fallen log and taken turns jumping off it into the grass. "We, like, had a contest to see who could jump the farthest. Evie won," she said, pointing to the tall, copper-haired girl.

The next girl, except for the red hair, was almost identical to the first in clothing, hair, and makeup. In his six months of parenting experience, Spence had visited the middle school enough to know that girls this age wanted nothing more than to look exactly like each other. Same straight hair, heavy eye makeup, jeans, and those open-buttoned shirts with the tank—no, that cami thing—beneath.

Spence cleaned the redhead's poison ivy, all the while wondering if any of these girls would become friends with Alyssa. If Alyssa would let them get close. If his niece would let anyone get close.

He finished with a Hispanic girl with large brown eyes and braces and the copper-haired girl named Evie; then it was Wonder Woman's turn to perch on top of the exam table.

She extended a lily white arm that looked as though no SPF sunscreen would be able to keep it from burning. Spence figured she'd be back in his clinic within the next forty-eight hours, wondering why her skin was lobster red.

A huge red bubble, about the size of a half-dollar, covered the soft skin on the inside of her arm. It probably itched like the devil, but the woman met his eyes without flinching when he doused it with the gel.

"That one is going to burst open and ooze," he warned her. "I'm going to go ahead and wrap it up now."

"Thank you," Deena said.

He pulled out a Coban bandage and some gauze pads. It occurred to him that this was a perfect opportunity to talk to Alyssa's cabin counselor, just to make sure she was on top of things.

"Girls," he said, "I need to talk to Miss Deena in private. Why don't you go next door to the commissary and get some candy. Ask Miss Suzie to put it on my tab."

The girls shot out of his clinic like sprinters out of the blocks. Good. He wrapped the gauze around the blistered patch on Deena's arm. "So—you have much camping experience?"

"None," Deena said.

Spence slowed his work as another red flag went up. "But you have a lot of experience with kids, right?"

"Not really."

He stopped bandaging her arm. "But you have some experience with kids."

"Well, I was a kid a long time ago. And I'm an aunt."

Spence frowned. Until six months ago, he'd been an uncle—a rather uninvolved uncle—so this didn't build credibility in his eyes. "So how did you happen to end up being a camp counselor?"

"Oh, it's a long story."

"I have time."

Deena raised an eyebrow. Not one of those overly plucked eyebrows that a lot of women favored, but a real eyebrow. A strong, arched eyebrow. "What is it, exactly, that you want to know?"

"I'm just trying to get to know you a little better." He cut the Coban and pressed it flat. "It's just that my. . .well, Alyssa, she's been through a lot." He hesitated, dreading this next part but knowing he had to tell her for Alyssa's sake. "She lost both her parents in a car accident six months ago." He kept his voice steady and ignored the sharp prick the words made in his heart. "It's been kind of rough."

Deena nodded sympathetically. "I'm so sorry. Pastor Rich discussed this a little with me when he went over cabin assignments." A trace of a smile softened the corners of her mouth. "If it eases your mind to know more about me, I'm thirty-five years old and have a PhD in pharmacology. I work at the University of Connecticut as a researcher in the Health Center. Breast cancer is my field. I'm not a medical doctor, but I'll take good care of her."

Spence cleaned the blistered patch on her leg and tried to sort out his thoughts. He respected Pastor Rich but still felt a bit uneasy with the camp director's decision to place Alyssa with Deena. He liked that she had a PhD but worried about her lack of experience with kids. "Alyssa's fragile. She's got moderate asthma and a list of allergies a mile long. Sometimes she forgets to take her medicine, so please be sure she comes to see me twice daily."

"Twice daily," Deena repeated.

"And keep her out of the pool today so the poison ivy has a chance to start drying up. Oh, and make sure she stays hydrated and wears sunscreen. She's quite fair-skinned."

"Got it." Deena hopped off the table. She had to be close to six feet tall, and when she put her hands on her hips, he couldn't help but imagine her in the red boots and Wonder Woman corset. He had to stop thinking about her like that. "Anything else?"

"No." *Yes.* A hundred other things flashed through his brain. Things like Alyssa would eat the treetop of her broccoli spear but not the trunk and no other vegetable. Like she was half blind without her glasses and not especially good-humored in the morning. She disliked his choice of music and sneezed when his dog entered the room. In short, Alyssa hated him, hated living with him, and did everything in her power to let him know it.

He stared at the woman in front of him, wanting to lay this knowledge at her feet in the hopes that she could somehow fix things, but he knew it would do absolutely no good. Unfortunately, Deena had even less experience with kids than he did.

"You're staring."

Spence pulled out his best grin. "I was just thinking that before you leave I should print out a picture of what poison ivy looks like. You know, just in case you happen to see it again."

Deena stiffened slightly. "I may be rusty on classifying plants, but I don't need a photograph." Back straight, she marched from the room in a huff.

When he'd insisted that Alyssa attend this camp, he'd been picturing someone else entirely in the role of cabin counselor. In his mind's eye, he'd pictured a woman with the godliness of Mother Teresa and the maternal skills of June Cleaver.

Instead, he'd gotten Wonder Woman meets Madame Curie. He struggled to conceal a wave of disappointment. Just what was God thinking, sending a scientist into Alyssa's life?

four

Deena bit into a slice of leathery bacon. She and the girls were sitting on the long, hard benches in the cafeteria. They'd been late to breakfast, and as a result, everything had been left under the food warmers far too long.

"Please pass the syrup, Aunt Deena," Evie asked and proceeded to flood her plate with the sugary liquid.

Deena considered warning Evie of the dangers of eating too much sugar but instead put a forkful of cold and rubbery scrambled eggs in her mouth.

Her arm itched, her new shorts were giving her a wedgie, and she had the beginning of a headache. Plus she felt like an idiot. How could she have led the girls through a patch of poison ivy? Here it was, only day two, and already she'd landed herself and the girls in the clinic.

She jumped as the sudden blare of a loudspeaker urged the campers to the amphitheater for morning devotions. She glanced at her half-eaten plate. No big loss. She could always ask Taylor for some candy. The girl had everything from Tic Tacs to Godiva stashed in her suitcase.

Following the crowd of boys and girls, Deena marched out of the building into the warm June sunshine. They passed a courtyard area with pots overflowing with geraniums and baby's breath. Several benches were situated beneath leafy green trees. She would love to bring some medical journals and spend hours in the shade reading. Not this morning, though. She followed the kids down a flagstone path to an outdoor theater.

Rows of rough-hewn benches lined a gentle slope that led to the shores of Lake Waramaug. In the early morning sun, the surface gleamed like polished silver. She could see the boathouse on the left-hand side and rows of kayaks laid out on the beach area.

Two teenagers with hair curling around their ears took their places on the wooden platform in front of the lake. Deena looked at their electric guitars and expected a slightly jazzed-up version of a traditional church song.

However, the first chord—played at a volume that made her teeth vibrate—told her there would be no rendition of "How Great Thou Art."

She gripped the edge of her seat as the music blasted through the outdoor stage. The pounding bass hummed through her like a heart resuscitator as the teens belted out a song that consisted of basically one lyric: "I will wait upon the Lord."

The kids around her began to clap and sing. When Deena had been their age, she'd loved being in the church choir. But then her mother had gotten sick and there hadn't been time or energy to bring Deena to practice. Afterward, Deena had not had the heart.

The song ended and Pastor Rich stepped onto the stage. His bald head gleamed in the sunlight. "God, we thank You for bringing us to this place where we can learn more about You. We ask Your blessing on this camp, that during this week we may see You. May we know Your presence with a depth and intimacy that we have never experienced as an individual and as a camp family before."

As the pastor continued to speak, Deena's chest tightened. She hadn't expected this. Hadn't expected that the sight of all these kids bowing their heads in prayer would make her skin tingle and her heart ache. They were so young and so beautiful, these kids, and she could almost feel the purity of their faith rising off them. It reminded her of what she had been like at this age. Her mother had been recently diagnosed with cancer, but Deena had been so sure God would cure her mom that it hadn't bothered her much. She had bent her head, just like these kids were doing now, and confidently thanked God for the healing He was about to bestow on her mother.

The pastor kept talking, but Deena couldn't focus. She kept remembering, fast-forwarding in her mind the course of her mother's illness and the strength with which Deena had held on to her faith. Right up until the week before her mother passed away, Deena had been convinced that God would spare her. When He hadn't, she felt like something had died inside her, right along with her mother.

She'd been to services since then. Not as often as she should have and mostly to please Stacy. She had not, however, asked God for any more miracles.

She couldn't bear to be here another second. It just hurt too much. Hunching over so as to draw as little notice to herself as possible, Deena left the benches and walked away.

Seeking the solace of an empty cabin, she had to put on a good face when she discovered she wasn't the only one who had skipped out on the morning service.

Allergy Girl lay on top of her bunk, her hands behind her head, her eyes closed.

"Alyssa? Are you okay?" Deena hurried to the girl's side. "Is it the poison ivy?"

"I don't think so. I think it's my allergies." The small girl coughed dryly, but the sound had a fake, forced quality to it.

Deena studied the girl's face. It was pale, and dark shadows rimmed her eyes, a classic sign of allergies. However, all Deena's instincts were telling her the girl's problems had nothing to do with dust in the cabin or the pines around them. She needed to draw the girl out and find out more. But how? Alyssa looked like she wanted to take a nap, not have a heart-to-heart.

What would Stacy do? Probably pull out her mixer and bond as they made chocolate chip cookies. Deena didn't have a kitchen to work in, and even if she did, she couldn't bake.

"Well," Deena said, "maybe you just need to rest for a bit. We all had a bad night."

The girl turned her head toward the wall. Deena studied the curve of her back. Stacy would probably sit beside the bed and rub the girl's shoulders.

Deena crossed the room to the dresser and pulled the cloth cover off Mr. Crackers's cage. The African Grey looked at her. "Good morning, Mr. Crackers," she said. "Welcome to Camp Bald Eagle."

The bird stretched his wings and shifted on the perch. He seemed to have traveled well—only a few extra feathers at the bottom of his cage suggested any stress. Deena opened his cage and pulled out his water container.

"You want some fresh water?"

Silence.

"Okay. You're giving me the silent treatment," Deena said, rinsing out the water dish in the bathroom sink. "Well, you could have been left at home. Andres wanted to take care of you, you know."

She gave the parrot the water. "Come on," she coaxed. "Shake your groove thing," she sang.

The bird just looked at her.

"Is that the only thing he knows how to say?"

Surprised, Deena turned to find Alyssa watching them. "Oh no, he knows a lot of words. But right now he's sulking because I kept his cage covered up most of yesterday."

"He's so pretty."

"Pretty bird," Mr. Crackers said.

Alyssa almost smiled but quickly scowled instead.

"Pretty bird," Mr. Crackers said, cocking his head from side to side.

"He likes you," Deena said, turning back to the bird. "He only talks to people he likes." She hesitated. "You want to help me feed him?"

"I guess," Alyssa said. Although her voice suggested she couldn't care less, she lost no time getting out of her bunk.

Deena had saved some fresh fruit from breakfast in her fanny pack. Pulling out a bunch of grapes, she handed one to Alyssa.

The girl carefully pushed it through the bars of the cage. For a moment, the parrot and the girl studied each other, and then the bird gently pecked the fruit from the girl's fingers.

She handed Alyssa another grape, and again the bird delicately took it. Alyssa turned to her, solemn as a judge, and said, "I've read that African Grey parrots are really smart."

"They are," Deena replied. "Mr. Crackers knows hundreds of words. He even speaks words in five languages."

"Out," Mr. Crackers said, fixing his gaze on Deena as if he were hoping to establish a telepathic connection.

"Oh, all right." Deena opened the cage and offered her arm to the parrot, who promptly hopped onto it. She withdrew the bird so Alyssa could stroke his feathers.

"He's so soft."

"He likes it when you stroke his back. Like this."

Alyssa repeated the gesture carefully. "Knee-how," she said. "That's 'hello' in Chinese."

"Weintraube," Mr. Crackers said. "Weintraube."

Deena sighed. "That's German for 'grape.' I should have left him at home, but he has abandonment issues complicated by low self-esteem." She looked at Alyssa for the first time. There were twin spots of color on the girl's cheeks. "Hey, would you like to hold him while I clean his cage?"

"I guess," Alyssa said and then immediately reconsidered. "I mean no. No thanks. What exactly do you mean, abandonment issues?"

"Well," Deena said and fed the parrot a grape. "I adopted Mr. Crackers from one of my colleagues who took a field assignment in New Zealand. Mr. Crackers was very attached to Dr. Carnado, and after he left, Mr. Crackers got very depressed." Alyssa stroked the bird. "He started acting out—saying inappropriate words and pecking and clawing."

"So what did you do?"

"Well, I wore gloves whenever I worked around him, and I tried to give him a lot of positive reinforcement. Boost his confidence."

"And he came around?" There was no disguising the interest in Alyssa's voice.

"Yes, but slowly." Deena faced the girl. "He has two large cages, one at work and the other at home." She touched the metal bars of the travel cage. "I take him back and forth in this one. He still gets afraid, though, about being abandoned again. That 'shake your groove thing'—if he's scared, he likes to sing that."

Alyssa edged closer and held out her thin white arm. "I guess I could hold him, Miss Deena. Just while you clean his cage."

The arm didn't look strong enough to hold a sparrow, much less a big bird like Mr. Crackers, so Deena settled the parrot on Alyssa's shoulder instead. As she worked, two sets of eyes followed her every movement. "I want to tell you," Deena said slowly, "that when I was sixteen, I lost my mom to cancer. My dad had a heart attack five years later. I know what it's like to lose your parents. If you ever want to talk about it, Alyssa, I'll listen. Anytime, day or night."

Alyssa frowned and studied her hands. Deena feared she'd said the wrong thing, but then Alyssa looked up. "Everyone wants me to talk about what happened, but I don't know what they want me to say."

Deena nodded. "My sister and I used to say the same thing. Some people seemed more curious than sympathetic, but either way, we just ended up thanking whoever it was for asking about our mom and then changing the subject. I'm telling you about my mom, Alyssa, not because I want you to tell me anything. But I want you to know that I'm here for you, and I've been through losing a parent. Sometimes it does help just to talk. Having my sister was a huge help to me."

Silence.

Deena changed the position of one of Mr. Crackers's toys in the cage. "Day or night. You can come to me. Now, do you want to see Mr. Crackers solve his puzzle ball?"

Behind those Clark Kent glasses, Alyssa's eyes blinked

furiously. She seemed surprised by the change in topic and took a moment to gather her thoughts. "Why did you ditch the morning devotional? Were you checking up on me?"

It was Deena's turn to feel her thoughts tumble and toss about in her mind. She could tell Alyssa that cabin counselors weren't required to attend morning devotions or say that Mr. Crackers had needed her attention. But one look at Alyssa's bright green eyes and she knew the girl would instantly recognize an evasion. She held the girl's gaze. "I wasn't checking up on you. I wanted to be alone for a bit. But I'm really glad you were here."

The girl's brow wrinkled as she considered Deena's words. "You think we'll get in trouble for ditching?"

Deena shook her head. The cage was clean now, but she wanted to give Mr. Crackers and Alyssa a little more time together. "No. We have about an hour or so before we're due at the zip lines."

Alyssa's gaze slid past Deena. "I think I'd rather just stay here in the cabin. My allergies are really bothering me."

"You can't stay here alone. But if you want, I could drop you off at the clinic. I'm sure your uncle wouldn't mind if you spent the rest of the day with him."

Alyssa pushed a strand of hair behind her ear. "Actually, Miss Deena, I'd rather do the zip lines."

Their eyes met. Alyssa seemed to be holding something back. Deena was intrigued but sensed now wasn't the time to push. Earning the girl's trust would require a lot of patience. Fortunately, in Deena's line of work, she had learned that some answers, no matter how badly you wanted them right away, took time.

five

"Weren't the zip lines totally cool, Miss Deena?" Britty asked with a flip of her long blond hair.

It was midafternoon, and they were waiting for their turn on the Leap of Faith, which, from the looks of those twin telephone poles and safety netting beneath, promised to be as scary as the zip lines had been.

Deena fanned her face and pulled her bottle of sunscreen from her fanny pack. They'd all been sweating, and there was no shade whatsoever. "Cool?" She shook her head. "More like terrifying."

Squirting a bit of the lotion into her hand, Deena insisted the girls all reapply. They grumbled, especially Britty, who claimed it kept getting into her eyes and messing up her makeup. "You'll thank me when you're thirty-five and have beautiful skin," Deena pointed out.

"You didn't look scared on the zip lines," Taylor said. "You were smiling the whole way."

"I wasn't smiling. I was gasping for air and dealing with the worst wedgie of my life. That harness was not meant for women my size."

The girls laughed. The line shuffled forward as another child successfully completed the jump from the top of the first telephone pole to the hanging trapeze.

"I can't wait to try the Leap of Faith." Next to her Evie practically vibrated with excitement. "Look how high up it is. It's going to feel like flying. You gonna do it, 'Lyssa?"

The small blond nodded. "Yeah. It looks like fun."

Fun wasn't the word for this activity, but it got her thinking. When was the last time Deena had done something just for fun? Last Christmas Dr. Chin, her boss, had a pizza party for the lab, but Deena had been staining some cells with a new batch of inhibitors and had missed half of it.

"Hey, 'Lyssa," Evie said. "Isn't that your uncle?"

Deena looked behind her, and there, indeed, was Spencer Rossi walking toward them. Just the sight of him set Deena's teeth on edge, although she wasn't quite sure why. Maybe because he needed a haircut. His blond hair curled over his ears, and he hadn't shaved this morning. Golden bristles, these a shade darker than his hair, covered his jawline.

"Hey," Spence said. "A girl jammed her finger on the volleyball courts, and I just finished taping it up. I saw you over here and figured I'd see how you guys were doing."

More like he was checking up on them. On her. Deena stiffened. "We're doing fine."

To Deena's surprise, Alyssa inched closer to her. She had the feeling the girl wasn't moving closer to her as much as she was moving away from her uncle.

"The Leap of Faith looks cool, doesn't it?" Spence said enthusiastically. "Would you guys mind if I did it with you?"

Deena watched Alyssa's face go so completely blank that she figured it had to take enormous effort to make it look like that. "Don't you have to get back to the clinic?"

"Miss Miriam is covering for me." He patted the cell phone strapped to his belt. "She'll call if she needs me."

Deena didn't understand the dynamics of the relationship between Spencer and Alyssa and figured time together might enlighten her. "The more the merrier."

The line moved forward. Taylor blew a bubble with her gum and dodged Evie's efforts to pop it. Lourdes speculated with Britty whether one of the rubber bands on her braces had snapped free during the zip lines or if she had swallowed it. Alyssa studied the ground as if the packed earth was the most interesting thing she'd ever seen.

"This doesn't look hard, Alyssa," Spence said gently. The girl didn't reply. Her gaze remained fixed on the ground, and she gave no indication that she had even heard him.

"Alyssa," Spence said. "There's nothing to be scared of."

"Well, you go first, then," Deena told him, trying to lighten the moment. "That way I can see if the pulley system is strong enough to hold you. If it doesn't collapse, it'll hold me."

The other girls laughed. "That's so cool that you do stuff like this, Miss Deena," Taylor said. "The only thing I do with my parents is shop or go out to dinner."

Britty said, "Your point?"

Everyone laughed again. Everyone but Alyssa, who had begun tracing a half circle in the dirt as if she wished she could dig a hole and simply disappear.

Soon it was their group's turn. True to his word, Spence went first. He climbed the telephone pole hand over hand, rung by rung, not hesitating as he pulled himself onto the top. For a moment he balanced on top of the pole, silhouetted by the pale summer sky, impossibly tall and athletic, his blond hair shades lighter than his deeply tanned skin.

Deena felt her stomach tighten at the sight of him up there—like a big, tawny lion about to spring. She didn't like this feeling, not at all. She'd made a rule not to date anyone she worked with and then made sure she didn't meet anyone outside of work. The rule had worked well, or so she'd thought.

She could see now that all those pesky little dating hormones had been collecting, building up in her system, and just waiting for the worst possible moment to make themselves known.

He waved down at them, and then like a competitive swimmer, he dove off the top of the pole. He soared though the air, arms outstretched like Superman. He caught the trapeze easily, and everyone cheered. Well, almost everyone. Deena didn't know whether to ignore Alyssa's shutdown or draw her out.

As Evie began her climb up the telephone pole, Spence rejoined them in the line. He wasn't breathing hard, but his face was flushed and there was a hint of sweat around his hairline. "It's really, really fun," he said. "Just don't look down, Alyssa, and remember there's a safety net under you. There's no way for you to get hurt."

"I don't want to do this anymore," Alyssa stated matter-of-factly. "I want to go back to the cabin."

Spence placed his hand on the girl's thin shoulder. He used his other hand to point to Evie. "Just look at Evie. She's having a great time, and so will you."

True enough, Evie seemed to be making steady progress up the telephone pole.

"I just don't want to do it." Alyssa's gaze found Deena's. "Do I have to?"

"Of course not," Deena said.

Spence shot Deena a dark look. "Just try it," he urged. "If you climb up partway and change your mind, you can always come right back down."

Alyssa shook her head. "I don't like heights."

Deena didn't think this statement was entirely true. The girl had shown no fear on the zip lines. Also, Alyssa seemed to have been looking forward to trying the Leap of Faith until her uncle had appeared. She decided to follow an instinct. "Well, I don't like heights, either. In fact, my stomach is still woozy from the zip lines. Every time I burp, I taste cheeseburger. Maybe I'll just sit this one out with you, Alyssa."

The girl looked at her gratefully, but Spence shot Deena another look that all but shouted she should stay out of this. "Sometimes the best way to get over a fear is to face it. That's what this exercise is all about—finding out how to let go of fears. There's no way you can get hurt, Alyssa. I promise you. And I'll be right here. Just try, honey. Please try."

"No!" Alyssa's face flushed, and her breathing quickened. The change happened quickly. One minute she seemed fine, just a little upset, and then the next, every breath seemed short and ineffective, as if her lungs were full of holes. Even before Spence's voice barked out an order to get the rescue inhaler, Deena's hand was inside her fanny pack drawing out the albuterol. She handed it to the girl, who stuck the plastic nozzle into her mouth and sucked the medication into her lungs.

Deena studied Alyssa's face more closely, frightened by what she'd seen and uncertain if the treatment was working and what she would do if it didn't. Fortunately, it did seem as if Alyssa were breathing a little more easily.

"Aunt Deena! Aunt Deena!"

She straightened slowly and turned. Her niece dangled from the trapeze, staring straight down at her. "Did you see me?" Evie yelled. "Did you see me? I did it!"

Unfortunately, Deena hadn't. She'd been too busy taking care of Alyssa. "I'm sorry." She wanted to explain that Alyssa had an asthma attack, but shouting it to the world would be embarrassing to Alyssa. She couldn't very well ask Evie to redo her jump, either.

"I'm sorry," she said again. "I bet it was a really great jump."

"Yeah," Evie said in a voice that almost, but not quite, masked her disappointment. "It was."

six

Deena dreamed of her mother. And in the dream, like so many others, Deena promised to use her life to help other women with breast cancer. She leaned over the hospital bed. *"I'll miss you,"* she said. *"I won't forget you. And I'll always love you."*

In the dream, her mother pushed back the long strands of Deena's hair, strands Deena had been hoping would soon grow long enough to cut and make into a wig for her mother. *"My special, shining girl,"* her mother whispered. *"So brave and so smart. God has blessed you so you can bless others."*

Deena jerked awake. For a moment, she didn't know where she was—if she had been dreaming or if something had actually brushed against her forehead. She sat up as high as the bed would allow in the low-ceilinged room and strained to see in the small amount of moonlight streaming through the window.

For a moment she saw only the dark outlines of the bunks and the boxy shadow of Mr. Crackers's cage atop the dresser. And then. . . her heart skipped a beat when something cold and clammy brushed against her calf.

She jerked her leg back and swallowed a scream. Fumbling in the darkness, she pulled out the flashlight tucked next to her pillow.

Clicking on the beam, she lifted the covers. A pair of small black eyes stared out of a fist-sized lump. Deena relaxed. A frog? Someone had put a frog in her bunk bed?

How old was that prank?

She spotted another one. It crouched near the first one. Poor thing. It looked scared to death. She reached to rescue it. Her fingers closed around the plump, moist body. She didn't want to crush it, so she kept her fist loosely closed.

Too loosely closed, it turned out. The frog slipped through

her fingers and leaped into the darkness.

Seconds later a single scream, as shrill as a whistle, pierced the darkness. And then everybody was screaming.

They were the loudest, most ear-piercing screams Deena had ever heard. Anyone who heard the girls would think something awful was happening, like they were being chopped to pieces by an ax murderer.

Scrambling down the rungs, Deena nearly fell in her haste to get down. "Take it easy, everyone." Her words were lost as another wave of screams shook the cabin walls. "It's only a frog."

"Frogs!" Lourdes screamed, tossing her pillow and blanket off the top bunk bed. "In my bed!"

"Eww," Taylor shrieked. "Mine, too!" The girl leaped from the top bunk and landed with a loud *thump* on the wood floor.

"Mine, too," Britty hollered. "Help!"

"Calm down, everyone!" Deena screamed as pillows and bedding sailed through the air.

Something crashed. Someone grabbed her around the waist and screamed in her ear. Deena lurched toward the light switch, hampered by the girl with the death grip around her waist.

"It's okay," Deena shouted and winced as someone stepped hard on her foot. "You're making it worse by screaming." She doubted anyone heard that, either.

Dragging along the girl clinging to her middle, she made it to the front wall and flicked on the switch. What she saw almost made her want to turn the light off.

Total chaos.

Girls screaming. Frogs jumping up all around them like popping kernels of corn. Pillows and sheets everywhere.

"Get it off me!" Taylor yelled, shimmying wildly as Britty whacked her back with a pillow.

"Hey, don't hurt it." Deena stepped forward to help. Too late—the frog sailed through the air and landed with a heavy *plop* in front of Alyssa.

The girl opened her mouth and froze. Deena couldn't tell if she was breathing or not.

She lurched toward Alyssa, hampered by Lourdes, who continued to hang on to her, begging her not to move.

"Calm down, everybody!" Deena knew she didn't sound so calm herself. She couldn't help herself. Things never got out of control in her laboratory.

I am so over my head, Deena realized. *So very over my head. I never should have come here. What was I thinking?*

Britty climbed onto the dresser, only to leap off shrieking. Mr. Crackers's bag of gravel overturned, and she heard the contents spill onto the floor. Mr. Crackers began to screech.

"I'll help you, Alyssa," Evie yelled, surging forward in an attempt to capture the frog that had Alyssa pinned against the wall. Her movement, however, only caused the frog to leap toward Alyssa, who shrieked in horror and then promptly burst into tears.

Deena finally reached Alyssa's side and tried to pull the girl's hands away from her face. "Alyssa, are you okay? Talk to me, honey!"

Alyssa looked up, her face chalk white. "I'm. . . Inha. . ."

"Hang on, honey," she said, "I'll get your inhaler."

She was halfway across the floor and picking up speed when suddenly the door shuddered under the force of someone pounding it with fists. A man's voice shouted, "What's going on in there? Is everyone all right?"

Deena grabbed Alyssa's albuterol inhaler. "We're okay," she yelled.

"I'm coming in!" the man yelled again.

She recognized that voice. "Don't. We're fine!" Deena placed the inhaler in Alyssa's hands and supervised as the girl brought it to her mouth, pushed the button, and inhaled.

"I'm counting to five," the man yelled.

"Girls," Deena ordered, "get dressed—fast. The cavalry's here!"

seven

The door opened. Deena, wearing navy sweats and a pair of pink bunny slippers, stood illuminated in the backlight of the cabin. "Hello, Spencer," she said cheerfully as if she'd run into him at the grocery store. "Nice to see you again."

" 'Nice to see you again?' " Spence narrowed his gaze. "Deena, it sounded like something terrible was going on here. Is everyone okay?"

"Everyone is fine." Her gaze strayed past him to the small group of camp counselors and campers that had gathered behind him. "Thanks for coming, everyone," she said, "but everything is fine. Sorry for all the noise."

She started to close the door, but Spence put his hand on the frame. "You can't do that—scare everybody like that and then just say it was nothing." He gestured behind him. "You worried a lot of people." Including himself.

He'd just been finishing up treating a kid who had spiked a fever of 102 in a nearby cabin. But even if he'd been in his own cabin halfway across the camp, he would have heard those screams. He was only surprised that more people hadn't come running.

"I'm sorry," Deena repeated more loudly this time. "We had a small problem with frogs, but it's completely under control now. Thank you for coming to see if we were okay."

"Told you it was something with either bugs or frogs," exclaimed Jenny, the counselor in the cabin nearest to Deena's. "Okay, everyone," she announced. "Time to get back to our cabin."

Deena murmured good night and again started to shut the door. Before it closed, another scream ripped through the cabin.

"Everything is not okay. I'm coming in," Spence said.

"Okay. But be careful where you step. I don't want you to squish one."

She was concerned about frogs when the girls were screaming bloody murder? Still, Spence moved carefully, shuffling his feet as he entered the cabin. He took a deep breath and released it. Frogs had done this?

The room looked as if a small tornado had swept through it. Every bed had been tossed, and pillows and bedding covered the floor, not to mention what looked like a bag of gravel had spilled everywhere. His gaze rose to the top of one of the bunks where the five girls huddled, peering at him over the top wooden slat.

He counted heads. Everyone looked okay. Thank God. His gaze lingered on Alyssa, white-faced and breathing a little too fast. He saw the rescue inhaler in her hand, and his jaw tightened.

"Look out, Uncle Spence!" Alyssa called. A scream, so shrill that Spence's eardrums seemed to swell in his head, filled the room.

Three more frogs hopped past him. Another one sailed overboard from its hiding spot in one of the upper bunks.

Broom in hand, Deena was carefully flushing them out from beneath the beds and dresser. "Get the door," she shouted. He couldn't actually hear the words above the shrieking, but he read her lips. And he moved. Fast.

❧

It was about two in the morning before the cabin was straightened and officially declared frog-free. Even then the girls still seemed unsettled, reluctant to go back to bed, fearing that more frogs would come out of hiding.

Only after Spence promised to sleep on the front porch and keep watch did the girls allow themselves to be resettled in the bunks. He prayed aloud for them and let each girl add to the prayer if she wanted. To his disappointment, but not surprise, Alyssa remained silent.

He was still thinking about this as he settled himself on the front step on the porch. High above, bright stars burned in a pitch-black sky. Alyssa had shut herself off not only from him, but also from the Lord. Was he pushing too hard? Or not hard enough?

He breathed more deeply and more slowly and listened as hard as he could. Sometimes, and he could never force this, he would get a feeling, a stirring in his heart, and it would tell him what to do.

He sure wished it would speak to him now.

Instead, the screen door creaked open, and Deena joined him on the step. "You don't have to stay," she said. "They're all asleep."

Under the porch light, her blue eyes were black as onyx. She still reminded him of Wonder Woman, though. Only her eyes had shadows under them, and they reflected a vulnerability that wouldn't exist in a superhero. Superheroes didn't wear fluffy pink bunny slippers, either.

"I told them I'd stay," he said. "I don't mind."

"You won't be very comfortable out here."

"Had worse."

" 'Had worse.' " Deena gave a poor imitation of his voice. "You can stop the macho thing," she continued in her normal voice. "The truth is you're a softie. You don't want the girls to wake up and not find you keeping guard outside."

He shrugged. Alyssa needed to know that when he gave his word, he kept it, whether it was convenient or not. Trust was something you earned, and sleeping on the porch was a price he was more than willing to pay.

"Nice slippers," he said.

"Evie gave them to me last Christmas. In case you didn't know, she's my niece."

"Thought she had to be related. Looks kind of like you. Has your eyes."

Deena sighed. "That she does. Look, I'm sorry you had to come out here tonight. Things got out of hand."

It was exactly as he'd feared, but he found little satisfaction in being correct. Oddly, he wanted to reassure her. "I don't think you're the first cabin counselor who has ever dealt with a prank involving frogs."

Kids could be challenging. In his six months of parenting, he had a whole new appreciation of the art of raising a child. Especially twelve-year-old girls. He remembered the first day he had arrived at Alyssa's house to live with her, how the very sight of him had turned the girl's face ashen. Even before he opened his mouth, he'd been doomed to say the wrong thing. She'd run for her room within minutes. He'd thought it would get better. Prayed it would. So far it hadn't.

He was beginning to wonder if Alyssa would be happier with someone else. Her maternal grandparents had offered to raise her, but they lived in Texas—a long way from Connecticut. Besides, Evan and Mattie had made him Alyssa's legal guardian. He'd been honored, but baffled when they discussed their decision with him. "Why me?" he'd asked, thinking himself the least likely choice.

"Because you're her favorite uncle," Evan said and patted his shoulder. "And you've got the biggest heart of anyone in the family."

Before the accident he and Alyssa had enjoyed each other's company. Now, however, she wouldn't give him the time of day.

"My ears are still ringing from the screams," Deena said.

Spence smiled. "They were pretty loud."

This close Spence could see her nose was slightly too long and her mouth too wide for classic beauty. But it was a striking face. She was not the kind of woman who walked into a room and faded into the background. She probably scared off a lot of men with that straight, frank look. He wasn't intimidated, though. But then again, she was wearing pink bunny slippers.

"Who did it?" Spence traced a crack in the wood step. "Who do you think released all those frogs?"

She shrugged. "Does it matter?"

"Of course it matters. This sounds like a prank a boy would play. I'll check with the other counselors and see if we can figure out who did it."

"I don't think you need to do that."

"You saw someone?"

"Not exactly." Deena pulled her knees more tightly to her chest. The sweatpants rose, revealing a very trim pair of ankles. He moved his gaze back to her profile.

"But you think you know who did it."

"I think it was Evie. The wild child." Deena sighed. "That's why I'm here. I'm supposed to make sure Evie stays out of trouble."

Great. Not only did Alyssa have a counselor who had no experience with kids, but she was also bunking with a possible juvenile delinquent. Spence studied the shadows on the step. Maybe Alyssa should change cabins. "So if your niece released the frogs, what are you going to do about it?"

Deena shrugged. "Don't know. Guess I'll talk to her. Tell her that pranks can have pretty serious consequences."

"That's a good start," Spence agreed. "If you'd like, we could both talk to her."

"Thanks, but I think it's better if I sit down one-on-one with her."

Somewhere in the dark an owl hooted; then the night went still once more. Spence looked up at the stars. "Maybe she's the kind of kid who needs clear limits. State the rules, and if she breaks them, give her a consequence."

"So what kind of consequence should I give for putting frogs in the beds?"

Spence looked at her. "Push-ups."

"Push-ups?" Deena laughed in surprise. "What's that got to do with frogs?"

"Nothing." It did seem kind of absurd, and Spence found himself grinning sheepishly. "It's what my father gave out as punishment. I'd say ten should do the trick."

"You're serious? Is that how you punish Alyssa?"

"We haven't crossed that bridge yet. You can't punish a kid for not smiling, for not wanting to talk to you." He shrugged.

"Sometimes I wish I could, especially if it'd make her open up to me."

"She will, Spence. She's got a good heart. You should see her with Mr. Crackers."

"Mr. Crackers?"

"My parrot."

He frowned and tried to remember whether Alyssa was allergic to birds. "Why would you bring a parrot to camp?" How crazy was that?

"He has abandonment issues," Deena said, "complicated by low self-esteem. Alyssa helps me clean his cage and feed him every morning."

Spence pushed his hands through his hair. He didn't know what kind of abandonment issues a parrot might have and didn't care if the parrot had low self-esteem. He cared about Alyssa. "Parrots can scratch and bite."

"Mr. Crackers wouldn't hurt a flea. He and Alyssa seem to like each other. They're becoming friends."

Spence frowned. A parrot wasn't the kind of friend he had in mind for Alyssa. He'd been hoping she and Lourdes would become friends. Lourdes seemed as though she'd be a good influence on her. "What about the other girls? Is she making friends with any of them?"

"I think so," Deena replied. "Some things take time."

Sometimes people needed help to get where they needed to be. A gentle push. "But you're encouraging her to do things with them, right?"

"Oh yeah," Deena agreed. "This afternoon we all played shuffleboard. Alyssa and I discovered we both stink at it. We kept sliding our pucks into the grass."

"I didn't see her in the breakout groups after the evening devotional," Spence commented. "She was avoiding me, wasn't she?"

"I don't know." Deena sighed. "We both went for a walk. We bought some ice cream and watched the fireflies. I haven't seen them since I was a really little girl, and guess what?

Alyssa has never seen them."

It was a nice picture, but he pushed it firmly out of his mind. He would have much rather heard that Deena had attended the devotional with Alyssa. Counselors weren't required to attend these sessions—the church had pastors who led them—but he thought she should set a good example. "I would appreciate it," he said stiffly, "if you would encourage her to participate in the camp activities. She needs to be learning about the Lord. The only way she's ever going to get through this time in her life is if she turns to God."

"Spence, I don't think you can force that kind of thing on someone."

It was said gently, but it irked him all the same. This sort of answer wasn't acceptable, especially not from the woman who was supposed to exert a strong Christian influence on his niece. "I would think that someone in your position would welcome an opportunity to guide someone who obviously needs it."

She stiffened. "Guide, Spence, or drag them by force to God?"

"Of course not drag her, but don't be so quick to let her skip out." He paused. "This afternoon, for instance, when I was trying to get Alyssa to do the Leap of Faith, you didn't back me up."

"Spence, she started having an anxiety attack."

"Because she was afraid. She wouldn't have been afraid if you had agreed with me. If you had assured her that she could do it."

"Oh, that's a lot of rubbish," Deena stated firmly. "She started having an anxiety attack when you began pushing her. Before you came she said she was looking forward to doing it."

They were almost nose to nose, and the expression in her eyes told Spence she wasn't backing down. "Look, I just saw her with an emergency inhaler in her hand a little bit ago. Was that my fault, too?" He felt righteous anger creep into his voice. "I don't want to argue with you. I'm just asking you to do your job."

The frog thing hadn't been her fault, and he knew it. Before he could apologize, before he was sure he even wanted to apologize, she stood. The screen door screeched open. "Asking, Spence? Or telling?"

The screen door banged lightly shut, and the wooden one after it. He heard the latch click into place and then silence.

"Sometimes you have to push a little," he explained to the empty space beside him. He wasn't forcing anything on Alyssa. You didn't wait for a drowning person to call for help. You simply jumped in and pulled her out of the water. That's all he was saying. The trick to saving someone was to get there in time. You couldn't hesitate.

He'd tried that once, and he had failed miserably.

eight

After the morning devotion and quiet time, Deena and the girls returned to the cabin to change into bathing suits. Deena slathered everyone with sunscreen, treated five cases of poison ivy, then escorted them to their kayak lesson.

Morning sunlight filtered through the trees as they walked down the path to the lake. These pines were much bigger than the ones at home. Her condo had two carefully pruned blue spruces in the front yard. The association always decorated them at Christmas. They were pretty, but nothing, really, compared to the towering trees around her.

"Hey, Aunt Deena," Evie said, falling into step beside her. "Can we look for the eagle's nest today?"

The girl's energy was contagious. She looked adorable, still young enough to have a step that bounced, yet old enough you could almost see the woman she would become someday.

"What's this about you and that eagle's nest? You've been dying to see it ever since we got here."

Evie shrugged. "Well, it's how the camp got its name, after all. My mom told me about it when we signed up. And I dreamed that I was an eagle. I had these huge wings, and I could fly."

Deena tuned out the rest of a rather colorful dream that included Stacy sitting on eggs that hatched into birds with human faces. One of those, of course, was Evie, who was placed in a cage while the other hatchling got to stay in the nest.

She suspected her niece was embellishing as she went along. Instead of paying attention, Deena wondered how to broach the subject of the frog incident. She didn't have actual proof, and she doubted Evie would simply confess. As a result, Deena couldn't just punish the girl. At the same time, the very last thing she needed was to have the prank repeated.

"Look, Evie, I'm not accusing you, but if you had something to do with those frogs, you should know that a prank like that could have had bad consequences. We're fortunate Alyssa's panic attack wasn't worse than it was."

"If I did release those frogs, and I'm not saying I did, what would happen?"

Deena studied the pine needles on the path. "I would ask you not to do it again."

"But would I get grounded? Have to scrub toilets? Or—" She paused. "Would I get sent home?"

"It was a prank. I'd let it go. This time."

"Oh," Evie said, sounding oddly disappointed.

They stepped into the clearing. A coarse sandy beach stretched along the shoreline. Reaching out, the long L-shaped dock extended into the lake. A group of campers gathered near the shore where a man stood lecturing. A man she recognized only too well.

Spencer Rossi was not only the camp nurse but also the kayak instructor? Deena stifled the urge to turn around and head for the cabin. But he'd already seen her, and she wasn't about to let him run her off. Besides, after last night she wasn't letting Evie out of her sight.

Evie whispered, "Hey, Alyssa. Your uncle looks hot in a bathing suit."

Hot? Deena considered the man in front of her. Okay. He was hot. Not that she really cared. Because she definitely wasn't interested in him. She was only doing what scientists did best—observe and analyze.

Tell that to her heart. It was beating like crazy.

"Okay," Spence said. "Looks like everyone's here now and we can get started. Today we're going to learn to paddle open-seated kayaks. They're lighter and easier to maneuver than canoes."

He held up a green-bladed paddle. "This," he said, holding the paddle chest-high, "is your friend. You don't want to fight the paddle in the water, so you move your wrists like this." He made a paddling motion. "Your wrists should only bend side to side, not rotate up and down." Deena tried not to notice the way the motions made the muscles in his chest flex. "You use your legs, too, and slightly rotate your body."

As Deena struggled to process this information, he added, "Keep your distance from other kayaks. Do not stand up. Do not jump in the water. No playing bumper boats." She tried to tune out the rumble of his voice. It wasn't as if she were in the market for a man. Especially not someone like Spence. If she were going to go for a guy, she'd pick a nerd.

A nerd would be perfect because they would have intellectual conversations about medical ethics and technology breakthroughs. They wouldn't be distracted by rogue hormones racing through their bloodstream and wreaking havoc with their nervous systems, giving them sleepless nights and sweaty palms. She wiped her hands on her shorts. Just how tall was the man anyway?

"Okay, everyone," Spence said. "Get going." He clapped his hands. Everyone charged for a kayak. Everyone except herself and Alyssa.

"We could sit on the shore and watch," Alyssa suggested.

Although she and Spence had exchanged strong words the night before, Deena agreed that Alyssa needed to get involved in the camp activities. "Or we could be partners."

"Do you know how to paddle a kayak?"

"No, and once I got seasick on the kiddie boats at Lake Compounce."

Alyssa pressed her lips together. "Why would you want to go out in the kayak if you think it might make you seasick?"

"Good question," Deena said. "But you know what? Sometimes you'll miss all the fun if you just sit on the sidelines." Goodness, that was something Stacy might say. "Besides," Deena added, "you're about to get a huge lecture from your uncle if you don't get in the kayak."

It was true. Already Spence was giving them a funny look, as if he was wondering what was going on.

"I guess we could try," Alyssa said. "You've got my rescue inhaler?"

Deena patted her fanny pack. "Yeah."

They walked over to the one kayak that no one else had picked. Built almost like a canoe, the kayak was long and thin with small plastic seats in the front and back. Unlike the kayaks Deena had ever seen, this one was totally open. No skirt covered the lower portion of the paddler. She could see the entire interior of the kayak, including a big puddle in the bottom. Deena lifted one of the life jackets and studied the brown stains along the edges. She was supposed to wear this? She'd rather culture it in the lab.

But Spence was watching, so she wouldn't let herself flinch as she eased the clammy fabric around herself. It was hard to buckle—obviously no one with a bust had ever attempted to wear it—but Deena let out the straps and cinched herself in.

Vest on, Alyssa climbed into the front of the kayak. Deena grabbed the tail, or whatever it was called, and pushed it into the water. The lake, leg-numbing cold, made her feel as though she'd dunked half her body in a vat of rubbing alcohol. When they were knee-deep, she climbed inside and settled herself in the hard plastic seat.

Sunlight warmed Deena's face and the cool pool of water she sat in. She paddled a little faster, enjoying the way the small vessel cut through the water. She could practically feel all the endorphins released by the brisk exercise shooting through her body.

She and Alyssa paddled past the long arm of the dock and toward the middle of the lake.

Ahead she saw Evie and Lourdes. The two girls were working well together, and their kayak moved smoothly through the water. Paddling a bit faster, Deena managed to catch up to them. "Hey," she called. "Isn't this great?"

Evie grinned back at her. "I didn't know you could kayak, Aunt Deena."

"I didn't, either." Deena felt tremendously pleased to see the admiration in Evie's eyes.

"Hey, Aunt Deena! Race you to the buoys!"

In the distance, Deena spotted the two floating orange cones. She vaguely remembered Spence saying something about staying within the barriers. He hadn't said anything about racing, though.

"How about it, Alyssa? You up for it?"

The girl turned around. "If you want to."

Deena wanted Evie to think she was a cool aunt. She also wanted to make the activity fun for Alyssa. "I think we can take them."

The two kayaks drew alongside each other, and Evie counted down. The minute she said, "Go!" Deena paddled as fast and as hard as she could.

So did Evie and Lourdes. At first, more water was moving than kayaks as four double-bladed paddles thrashed. Screaming as the icy water sprayed over her, Deena dug her paddle into the water. The kayak responded sluggishly at first but then shot forward.

Another paddle full of water slapped her face. Deena laughed and leaned forward. Their kayak gained speed, but so did Evie's. The two boats stayed neck and neck as they raced toward the twin buoys.

Evie was screaming encouragement to Lourdes, who, with arms flailing, looked as if someone had pressed a button and sent her into fast-forward.

In the excitement Alyssa somehow was flicking more water back into the kayak and into Deena's face than she was helping move the boat forward. Doing her best to ignore the cold shower, Deena plowed forward.

The two kayaks drew even closer. They were so close Deena could have reached out and touched her niece's arm if she'd wanted to. Spence's warning—*"Keep your distance from other kayaks"*—rang in her ear, but she ignored it. They were having fun. Evie's paddle dumped even more water into her lap. That combined with the spray from Alyssa's furious paddling made Deena feel as if she were taking in as much water as the *Titanic*. She wanted to laugh so badly it took everything she had in her to keep paddling.

They were almost at the buoys, and the race was close. Then Deena felt something like a big fish smack her in the face. It stunned her for a second and hurt like crazy. She wanted to keep on paddling, but suddenly Evie was shouting, "Stop! Stop the race!" The girls slowed. "Aunt Deena, I am so sorry. Are you okay? It was an accident. I am so sorry."

"I'm fine." She still wasn't quite sure what had happened. Her face throbbed, and she tasted lake water. When she touched her check, however, her fingers came away sticky. Blood?

It dawned on her that it wasn't blood from a flying fish. It was her blood. Evie had clocked her with the paddle.

"You're not fine," Evie cried. "You're bleeding."

"Help!" Lourdes began to scream. "We need help!"

❧

It could have been worse, Deena reflected a short time later as she lay on the narrow examination table in Spence's clinic. She could have been knocked out of the kayak, and Spence might have had to jump in the water and rescue her. Put his arms around her. Perform CPR, even.

She would have hated that. Hugging and kissing people always made her uncomfortable. Yet when Spence bent over her, Deena's stomach gave a little flip-flop, and her heart felt like it shriveled to the size of a raisin. She should have insisted that he let Miss Miriam treat her. Instead, she hadn't even protested when Spence had told the gray-haired nurse that he would take care of her. Miss Miriam's gaze had gone from Deena's face to Spence's and then back to Deena's. She had then announced she was going on a coffee break and would be gone for thirty minutes.

Now she had to deal with her riotously pounding heart as Spence bent over her. This close she could see the pores in his skin. With his gaze locked on her cheek, she could study his eyes without his looking back into her own. They were forest green, the same rich color of pine needles.

Maybe CPR from this guy wouldn't be so bad.

Deena squashed that thought as quickly as it came.

"It's not deep, and you won't need stitches," Spence concluded, still nearly nose to nose. "The important thing is to keep it clean." He dabbed her cut with a sterile gauze pad. "You're going to have a bruise, though."

"I'm sure it's fine. Can I go now?"

"Not yet. We're dealing with lake water, you know."

Deena shuddered to think of all the bacteria, parasites, and other kinds of infections that might be lurking in the waters of Lake Waramaug. "It was worth it," she joked. "We almost won the race, you know."

"I saw." Spence dabbed antiseptic cream on her cheek. "And you were losing. If Evie hadn't clocked you with the paddle, you would have crashed into the buoy. I probably would have had to fish you both out of the water."

"I beg your pardon. Coming close to that buoy was the fastest way to the finish line."

The antiseptic cream burned against her skin. "Ouch!" She felt Spence's fingers hesitate before smoothing more of it into the cut.

"Thanks for the rescue, though. I have to hand it to you. I've never seen anyone paddle so fast in my life."

"I was motivated." He taped a bandage into place. "I thought something had happened to Alyssa." He met her gaze and grinned.

Sitting up, she swung her legs over the side of the table. "Thanks, Spence."

He shrugged. "You're welcome. I hope you're not planning on trying waterskiing, or the obstacle course, or horseback riding."

"You may think I'm not athletic," Deena said, "but yesterday I actually played two games of Ping-Pong and nobody got hurt."

Spence laughed. "I'm not sure Ping-Pong qualifies as an athletic event."

"That's because you haven't seen me play it." Deena stood. She was a tall woman, but even so, she had to look up to meet his gaze. "Well, I guess I'd better get ready for rock climbing this afternoon." It was a joke, but he didn't laugh.

She started to leave, and then Spence said, "Deena?"

She turned around. "Yeah?"

"I'm sorry about last night. I didn't mean to imply that you weren't doing a good job."

"I'm sorry, too. You made some good points."

He hesitated, and she could see him thinking hard about whether he should say something or not. She found herself leaning slightly forward. "I saw it happen," he admitted. "I knew it was you." He shifted, but his gaze stayed steady on her face. "The one who was hurt. Not Alyssa. I just wanted you to know that."

Her fingers touched the small bandage he had placed on her cheek. "That's what I thought," she said and then added softly, "but it's good to know. For sure, I mean."

They stood like that for a few seconds; then they both smiled at exactly the same time. And it felt foolish and silly and completely right to be looking at him the way she was.

"See you tonight at the campfire."

Deena's heart skipped into another gear. "Yeah, Spence," she said. "See you tonight."

nine

When Deena returned to the cabin, she found the girls sitting on the floor in a circle. Holding hands and with their heads bent, they obviously were praying. The back of her throat went tight. "Hey," she said softly.

As soon as Evie saw her, she jumped up and nearly knocked her over with a massive hug. The other girls quickly joined her. Straining for room, they wiggled closer and struggled to get their arms around her.

"Aunt Deena," Evie cried. "Are you okay? I've been so worried."

"I was, like, so worried, too," Britty said. Her eyes were large within their frame of glitter shadow and purple liner. "You were bleeding pretty badly."

"I screamed so loud for help," Lourdes informed her, "that I broke one of the rubber bands on my braces and swallowed it."

Before Deena could take this in, Taylor began talking about the blood on Deena's shirt.

"I guess I'd better change," Deena said.

The five sets of arms around her lessened their pressure immediately.

"I'm so, so sorry, Aunt Deena. I almost killed you."

"It would take more than a kayak paddle to kill me," Deena said cheerfully. "Besides, it was my own fault letting my kayak get so close to yours." She looked down at that copper-colored head bowed in shame. It was so beautiful, so precious, those corkscrew curls falling midway down Evie's back.

She remembered when Evie was a baby. The first time Stacy let her hold Evie, she was so small, so perfect. Deena had been astonished by the depth of love she felt for her niece. When she bent to kiss the top of Evie's silken head, Evie had howled like a banshee, and Deena immediately handed her back. She realized now that she had been handing her back to Stacy in one way or another all Evie's life.

"So you're not mad at me?" Evie stepped back to look at Deena's face.

"Not a bit," Deena said. "I love you, honey." When was the last time she had said those words to her niece? Or to Stacy? A long time, she realized. As a scientist, she had to be analytical, observant, detached. She supposed those qualities had slipped into her personal life.

Seemingly reassured, Evie stepped back. "We cleaned while you were at the clinic."

Deena looked around. The cabin's plank floors gleamed a soft honey color, the beds had been made, and the clutter of clothes lying on the floor had disappeared.

"It looks great," Deena said. "You even cleaned Mr. Crackers's cage."

"Alyssa did," Evie said. "I wanted to help, but Mr. Crackers tried to bite me. And he said a bad word, too."

"Several bad words," Britty confirmed. "We lost track of how many when he started speaking foreign languages."

"He wasn't being mean," Alyssa said. "He was speaking his fear language."

"Fear language?" Taylor stared at Alyssa. "What are you talking about?"

"When Mr. Crackers gets afraid, he shows it by biting and cursing," Alyssa explained. "But all you have to do to get him to stop is talk to him."

"He's a nasty bird," Britty said. "When I tried to talk to him, I think he pooped on purpose to gross me out."

Deena laughed. "He is a character. I'll give him that."

"I'd better give this back to you." Alyssa handed Deena her rescue inhaler. "I took two puffs."

"That's okay," Deena said. "You're feeling better now, right?"

"I guess."

"This place sure is clean. As clean as my lab. And that, by

the way, is always spotless. It has to be. Especially my cell culture room. We have a UV light that helps keep the area sterile."

"Cell culture room?" Lourdes asked. "What's a cell culture room?"

"It's a place where I examine tissue from people who have cancer. After a doctor does a biopsy on the patient, some of the tissue comes to us for research." Deena struggled to think in simple terms. "I isolate the cancer cells and try to figure out how to kill them in a way that they never come back."

"Are you really curing cancer like Evie said?" Taylor asked.

"I'm trying," Deena said, glad the conversation had shifted from her injury to her work. "So are a lot of really smart, dedicated people. We're making progress every day."

"Do you have test tubes of blood everywhere?" This came from Britty, who had equal parts fascination and horror on her face.

"How close are you to finding a cure?" Lourdes added.

Deena smiled. "We're a lot closer than we used to be. And no, I don't have test tubes with blood in them everywhere. All our samples are kept in the incubator—it looks kind of like a refrigerator or freezer, and it maintains a very specific set of conditions."

Deena checked her watch. "Hey, you guys are going to be late for your volleyball match. How about you head over there, and I'll take a shower and catch up with you."

The girls didn't need much convincing. The volleyball match was one of the coed activities scheduled, and the girls had been looking forward to it.

Deena took a quick shower and dressed in a pair of white shorts and a green sleeveless top. When she stepped back into the room, she saw Alyssa sitting cross-legged in front of Mr. Crackers's cage. "I hope you're not having a staring contest," Deena said. "Because Mr. Crackers always wins. He's pretty good at blinking games, too."

Alyssa looked up. Her eyes looked very green behind her

glasses. "Do you ever feel sorry for him? In that cage all the time? I mean, what does he do all day but sit on that perch and watch everyone? You ever wonder what he's thinking?"

Deena tossed her towel on the chair and crouched next to the girl. "It's all he's ever known, I guess. He'd die if he were released into the wild." She paused. "You don't miss what you've never known."

Alyssa's golden head shook in disagreement. "I don't think so, Miss Deena. He can look through those bars and see a whole other world out there—he can see it through the bars and hear it and smell it, but he can't be part of it."

What should she say? The bird had been raised in captivity. "He doesn't think like that," Deena said at last. "He's in a safe place, in his home."

"You think he ever misses his old life? The one he had with the guy who had him before you?"

Just where was all this going? What was it that Alyssa needed to hear? "No," Deena said. "Well, maybe at first he did, but then he discovered rock-and-roll music." She studied Alyssa's face, unsmiling and fixed on the bird, as if she expected at any moment Mr. Crackers would open his mouth and join the conversation. "He adjusted, Alyssa. It took time, but he's happy now."

Alyssa turned to her. "What if you don't want to be happy? What if you don't want to forget?"

Deena suddenly understood the reasons for Alyssa's questions—and some of her fears, too. It had nothing to do with Mr. Crackers and everything to do with the loss of her parents.

"You won't forget them," she said gently. "The being happy part—that one is harder. But one of these days, Alyssa, you're going to wake up and stop seeing the bars. You're just going to see the world."

"How do you know?"

"Because," Deena said slowly, "that's the way it happened for me."

ten

The marshmallow made a whooshing noise and then burst into flames. Deena pulled the stick from the fire and blew out the small inferno. The smoking remains looked like they'd disintegrate if she touched them.

"Spence," she said, holding the marshmallow up for his inspection. "I incinerated it."

Packed around the blazing campfire set in an open field, a group of campers stuck long skewers into the flames. Their faces glowed with excitement in the light of the fire as they laughed and held up their marshmallows, making designs with the smoke as if the skewers were Fourth of July sparklers.

"You didn't incinerate it," Spence said. "It's perfect."

"Perfect? Spence, it isn't even edible."

Spencer blew out his own blackened marshmallow. "You want it burned on the outside but soft and gooey on the inside. I'll show you."

He led her through the mass of kids waiting for a chance to toast their marshmallows to a table loaded with stacks of chocolate bars and graham crackers.

Deena copied what Spence chose and then followed him to the edge of the field where tall pines marked the beginning of the woods. They found a private spot beneath the base of one of the trees. They could still watch and hear the kids, but it was quieter. Deena began assembling her s'more. The marshmallow nearly burned her fingers as she pulled the charred remains off the stick. "It looks carcinogenic."

"Charcoal is good for digestion. Don't judge before you try it."

Deena doubted his statement greatly but smeared the marshmallow on top of the graham cracker and then added a few squares of chocolate. She added another graham cracker

58

and squished the concoction together.

"Go ahead," Spence urged, already crunching happily.

As a rule Deena stayed away from sweets. She tried to eat lots of fruits and vegetables and exercise regularly. She avoided red meat entirely and made sure she ate fish at least twice a week. However, since she'd arrived at camp, she'd blown her diet completely. One small cookie wouldn't make much difference.

She nibbled an edge. Not bad. She took a slightly larger bite and tasted the mix of sweet chocolate and gooey, sticky marshmallow.

"Like it?"

"Mmm. Love it." Deena polished off the rest of the cookie in three bites. Afterward she licked her fingers. "That is the most delicious thing I've ever eaten."

"You've never had one of these before?"

Deena shook her head. "My family was never into camping. My dad was more into intellectual outings like going to museums. And my mom, well, she was sick a lot."

She wanted another s'more but didn't want to move. "When I get back to my lab, I'll have to find a way to make these with a Bunsen burner. Or maybe the microwave."

In front of them the kids laughed, shouted, and teased each other playfully. The bonfire, smelling pleasantly of smoke and woods, sent up colorful flames that danced in the darkness.

"You can't make these in a lab and have them taste the same." Spence swatted a bug. "You have to be miles from civilization, looking up at the stars and listening to the night."

Deena heard the crackle of the fire, the laughter of the kids, the deep-pitched croak of the bullfrogs, and the plaintive *wra–a–a–ah* sound of the toads. She had to admit, he might be right. Not that she'd tell him that.

"I don't know, Spence, a burned marshmallow is a burned marshmallow."

"Not burned, toasted. Think of it as Cajun, but without the spices."

"It was burned, but that's actually good news for me because

I burn everything. Well, unless I can microwave it. I can't wait to tell Stacy I've actually found something that tastes great burned."

"Who's Stacy?"

"My younger sister. Evie's mother. She was supposed to be the cabin counselor, but she's in a high-risk pregnancy. That's how I ended up here."

"Oh, right—you told me about her the other night. How she's doing?"

"Talked to her yesterday. She and the baby are doing fine. She's decided that being at this camp is really good for me as well as Evie. She thinks I spend way too much time in my lab." Deena poked her empty skewer into a clump of pine needles and stirred them around.

"My brother, Evan, used to tell me I worked too hard," Spence said. "He thought I needed more fun in my life. He never understood why I would choose a job that didn't have regular hours."

"I do," Deena said in heartfelt understanding. "When people are depending on you, you owe it to them to work as hard as you can."

"You can't tell a person lost in the middle of a snowstorm to wait for Thanksgiving dinner to finish."

"Absolutely not," Deena agreed. "Am I supposed to say to some woman fighting for her life, 'Sorry, I may have found a new therapy for you, but I can't work overtime'?"

Deena jumped when Spence reached over and lightly slapped her arm. "Mosquito," he said in apology.

Someone started playing a guitar. She closed her eyes as the kids began singing "Lean on Me." It felt so right. Being there. She let herself shift slightly toward Spence. The kids' voices were so pure and beautiful. She had the strongest urge to lay her head on Spence's shoulder and for him to slip his arm around her. To let herself lean on him, just like the song said. Of course she wouldn't. "We're fortunate to have work we love to do," she said.

"Tell me about the lifesaving therapy."

She opened her eyes. "You want the whole story or the press release version?"

"The whole story, of course."

She settled more deeply into the tree trunk. "I want the same, then, about you." He nodded. "I'm into translational biology. That means instead of studying fruit flies or yeast, we study actual cancer cells. I'm studying all the pathways that cause cancer to grow."

As she spoke, she thought of Andres, Quing, Nrushingh, working even now while she was here. She wondered about the data they would have gathered by now and felt guilty because they were doing her work for her.

Spence listened and asked a lot of good questions, which drew Deena even more deeply into the discussion. It felt good to talk about her work with him. Stacy always enjoyed hearing about her work, but invariably something interrupted them. Jack wanted help with his homework, Evie had to be picked up or driven somewhere, or Jeff needed her.

"I'm sorry, Spence," she apologized, realizing they'd spent far too much time talking about her work. "I sort of got carried away."

"Don't think that," he said. "I liked hearing about it. My dad was a cardiac surgeon, and my brother was an optometrist."

She glanced at the dark outline of his profile. "And you became an EMT."

He snorted in amusement. "Much to my father's disappointment. He kept saying the pay was poor, the opportunity for advancement minimal, and the working conditions dangerous. In short, he thought I'd lost my mind."

Deena made a sympathetic noise. Her father had thought she was crazy to immerse herself in the disease that had killed her mother. "But you like it, right? Being an EMT?"

"Loved it. I quit about six months ago when my brother and sister-in-law died and I became Alyssa's legal guardian. Fortunately, I've had enough savings to be a stay-at-home dad. I can't do that forever, though."

"Well, it's good that you're doing it now."

It was hard to picture a big guy like him doing ordinary things like laundry and cooking, but she decided she liked learning about this homey side of him.

"It's been a real education," he said. "I took her shopping at the mall and discovered that buying a twelve-year-old clothing is next to impossible. Either the shirts have puppies on them, or they're way too clingy."

"Oh, Spence, couldn't you have asked your mom or a female friend to help?"

"I thought about asking one of Alyssa's friend's moms but figured the more time we spent doing stuff together, the better we'd get to know each other. But it didn't quite work out that way. We went to this one store that had lots of girlie clothes I thought Alyssa would like. I kept holding up shirts, asking if she liked them, and she kept saying no. Finally, she tried on this one shirt, and it was way too clingy. I had to shout to be heard above this awful rock music, and just as I opened my mouth, the music stopped and everybody in the store heard me. Alyssa turned red as a tomato and then insisted we leave."

When Deena stopped laughing, she turned to study his profile. "You were there with her," she said. "That's what's most important. She may not seem like she appreciates what you're doing for her, but deep inside she does."

Spence shrugged, and his mood turned more serious. "I know she's got a lot of stuff going on in her head and things won't get better overnight. But sometimes I wonder if she's ever going to be happy again."

"She will be," Deena promised. "She's lucky to have you, Spence. Not a lot of guys would give up a life they loved and relocate like you did."

"Not many people would step in at the last minute and take their pregnant sister's place as a camp counselor, especially when that person wasn't exactly the outdoors type."

"I know a lot about the outdoors. In ninth grade I got an A on my 'biology in a box' project. I identified all sorts of leaves and bugs."

"But not poison ivy," Spence teased.

"And now that I'm more familiar with it, I see it everywhere." Deena smiled wickedly. "I could be wrong, but just before you sat down, I thought I saw a very suspicious-looking patch of red-tipped leaves. Of course, I'm sure that an outdoors person like yourself would have recognized if it was poison ivy."

Although she'd been teasing, she enjoyed the way Spence jumped from his spot. Unfortunately, it placed him even closer to her. They were practically shoulder to shoulder. Worse, she couldn't move an inch without making it obvious that his proximity made her uncomfortable.

Worse still, he put his big, warm palm right on top of her hand. It covered hers completely. She stared at their hands, felt her heart start to beat so hard it seemed as if it would pound its way right out of her chest. It was ridiculous to feel this way about a total stranger. The problem was, he didn't feel like a total stranger.

She had that urge again to lay her head on his shoulder and just sit like that for a long time—just listening to the night and watching the kids playing around the campfire. She wanted to let down her guard and fully open her heart, something she'd never done with a man before.

At the same time, she knew the situation was impossible. She and Spence were completely wrong for each other. He had Alyssa, who needed everything he had to give. Deena, well, she had her work. She might have explained what she did, but it wasn't the whole story. She hadn't told him enough—not about her mother, her aunt, and her grandmother—and most important, not about herself.

The weight of his hand on hers began to feel more like a burden than a connection. She should tell him, right now, before this went any further.

Deena searched for the stars, barely visible in the vast pool of darkness. This was exactly why she didn't like to get to know anyone too deeply. Once you got past the casual what-do-you-do-for-a-living stage, the questions got harder. It was like one of those game shows on TV where the payoff grew with each question, as did the risk of losing it all.

She was not a gambler, and she had trained herself, so she thought, not to want things she couldn't have.

Sometimes a person had to carry around things that were hard to live with, but you did the best you could because you knew sharing them would only increase their weight. It wouldn't change things. It would only give someone else another burden to carry. And Deena had no intention of doing that.

eleven

Spence spent the morning stitching up a girl who had cut her leg on a rock in the tug-of-war pit, fishing a pretzel stick from the nasal passage of a boy who had placed it there on a dare, and cleaning the injury of a boy who had hooked himself in the shoulder while practicing casting.

By ten o'clock, he was ready for a break. He asked Miss Miriam to cover for him. She grinned and winked. "Heard your girl is on the archery field."

Spence grinned. "Figure I'll see if she can hit the target."

"Take your time, honey."

"Thanks." Spence pulled a brown lunch sack from the small refrigerator. "I'll be back in an hour."

On his way to the archery field, he passed the blackened remains of the campfire and smiled. He'd enjoyed seeing Deena eat her first s'more. Even more than that, he'd liked sitting beneath the tree and talking to her. He admired the work she was doing. She was a good listener, and he'd opened up to her more than was customary.

In the field he saw a line of archery targets and a group of girls standing in rows. Careful to approach from the side, Spence paused as arrows flew. Some actually hit the targets, but most sailed through the air and disappeared in the grass.

A moment later, a new row of girls stepped forward. He recognized Alyssa's small frame and honey-colored hair. He held his breath as she loaded the bow and pulled the string back. Sunlight reflected off her glasses, and the bow looked enormous in her small hands.

He laughed when her arrow landed about a foot from her. At least she'd tried.

Okay. Archery obviously wasn't her thing. A lot of things,

it seemed, weren't her thing. Even before the accident, she'd been kind of a quiet kid. Not a girlie girl and certainly not an athlete.

He remembered last Christmas when the family had gathered at Evan's house as they always did. Beneath an evergreen so high it touched the ceiling in the great room, there'd been a mountain of presents—skis, clothing, an enormous stuffed polar bear, and a girl's ten-speed mountain bike.

Alyssa, however, had been curled up in the window seat with *The Lion, the Witch, and the Wardrobe*. He had a feeling those ice skates he'd given her weren't going to get a lot of use. His niece was a bookworm.

Proposing a toast, Evan had proudly told him that Alyssa had tested into the district's gifted and talented program, which would allow her to learn with, as he put it, "nerds just like her."

Spence remembered his brother's flushed cheeks and too-bright eyes. He'd looked at the nearly empty glass in Evan's hand and remembered another Christmas and another glass in his brother's hand. Something in his brain had flashed a warning signal. He decided to discuss it with him later in private.

But the conversation had never happened. His brother and sister-in-law had died less than two weeks later. The crash had been ruled an accident, but alcohol had been involved.

Spence pushed the memory aside. Regrets were useless. What mattered now was Alyssa—that he was there for her in the way he hadn't been for his brother.

Maybe he couldn't give her back her father, but he could teach her how to shoot an arrow. When everyone paused to collect arrows, Spence stepped forward. As he did, he saw Deena.

She wore denim shorts and a camp T-shirt, yet even that simple outfit looked beautiful on her. The sight of those long legs and that ridiculously small waist made his mouth go dry.

He brought his gaze to her face but found no comfort there.

A small, colorful bruise stained her left cheek. It was slightly swollen and tender looking, but no sign of infection. "Hey," he said. "How're you doing?"

"So far so good," Deena replied. "This is a nice surprise."

"Yeah, well, I was just looking for a spot to eat my lunch." He held up the bag as if his words weren't proof enough—as if it wasn't obvious what he was doing there. "Hi, Alyssa." Spence tried to meet his niece's gaze. "I saw you trying. Good job."

"I stink at this."

"You're trying. That's all I care about." *And I want you to have fun, make friends, feel the sunshine on your face, and know that God has a plan for you.*

"Do I have to keep practicing? I've come closer to hitting my foot than I have the target."

Spence put his hand on Alyssa's shoulder. Although she flinched at his touch, he didn't remove it. "I'm sure you can learn. Let me show you."

"You'd better help my aunt Deena, too," Evie informed him, joining them from her place in the line next to them. Her copper eyebrows lifted. "She needs it even more than Alyssa."

"Evie," Deena said in a tone of warning. "You know I've been hitting the target consistently."

"Yeah," Evie agreed, grinning. "But not *your* target."

Deena smiled sheepishly at him. "I pull a little to the left." Her face had more color in it today—not counting the bruised area—and those light blue eyes twinkled.

"A *lot* to the left," Evie said. "People are jumping out of the way when they see you taking aim."

"Evie, that is such an exaggeration." But she was grinning, and so was Evie.

Spence wished he and Alyssa could joke like that with each other. He'd even be happy with a simple conversation as long as it was the real Alyssa talking, saying what she really thought instead of being so polite all the time.

"I'll help you both," he promised.

When it was Alyssa's turn, he stood behind her. Reaching

around her, he positioned her arms correctly on the bow. As usual, the size of her arms humbled him. He could have spanned the widest part with his thumb and index finger.

"Like this," he said, and, keeping his fingers over Alyssa's, he drew the string even tighter and then released the arrow. It flew through the air and speared the target. Not a perfect bull's-eye, but Alyssa almost looked him in the eye and said, "Good job, Uncle Spence."

"Thank you." And just that quickly the moment ended. Alyssa scooted off to stand beside Evie. He glanced at Deena, saw her nodding in approval. "Okay, Deena. How about you give it a try by yourself?"

Deena shook her head. "You don't have to teach me, Spence. I came here to watch. The girls talked me into trying."

"I've got the time." Spence handed her the bow. "Besides, you never know when your archery skills might come in handy."

Deena's arched eyebrows suggested that was about as probable as donkeys flying. "I don't anticipate needing to shoot a bow and arrow in my laboratory."

"The girls are watching us," Spence said softly. "If you don't let me teach you how to shoot an arrow, they're going to wonder why I'm standing here so close to you."

Those words got her moving. It wasn't flattering, but Spence had only been teasing. They both knew their time at the camp was limited. Soon she'd be returning to her research job, and he, well, he would return to Evan's house and continue to piece together his and Alyssa's lives.

He folded his arms as she drew back the bow. For a researcher who spent most of her days in the lab, she had nice biceps, and her triceps weren't half bad, either. "Tighter. Pull back tighter," he coached.

The bow strained tighter, and Deena released the arrow. It hooked left and landed dead center in the target next to theirs. Alyssa and Evie hooted with laughter. Spence felt his jaw drop.

"The same thing happened to me when we played shuffle-board," Deena admitted. "Everything went left."

"At least you didn't hit anybody," Spence said, deciding right then and there that he wasn't leaving until he was sure she could shoot an arrow straight.

As he had with Alyssa, he came up behind her to show her the proper way to hold the bow. The moment his arms went around her, he realized just how perfectly she fit into them. Those soft little spikes of hair just touched his chin, and the slightest trace of something fruity tantalized his nostrils.

"Now draw the string back," he said, wanting to draw her into his arms. It was all he could do not to nuzzle her ear.

The movement brought them even closer, aligning their bodies arm for arm, leg for leg, breath for breath. "And close one eye," he whispered because his voice had gone hoarse. Now the bow was definitely trembling. "Aim for the bull's-eye and. . .release."

Spence released his grip on the arrow and watched from above Deena's shoulders as the arrow sailed at least a foot over the top of the target. "At least it went straight," he said. His feet seemed to have grown roots.

"Yeah," Deena agreed, and her breathing sounded strained. "It went straight. Very straight."

"I think the problem was your elbow." He pushed the limb lightly against her hip. "You need to keep it lined up with your body."

The problem wasn't her alignment, though, and he knew it. No, the problem had nothing to do with archery, either. It was this attraction between them. He stepped away from her to get another arrow.

He'd come to the camp to bond with Alyssa, help bring her to God, not fall for Deena, no matter how attractive or smart she was, no matter how long it had been since he'd felt this way about a woman.

He'd been in relationships before. Not many, but enough to know the odds were slim that he and Deena would end up in a forever kind of relationship. There was Alyssa to consider as well. What would happen if he got involved with Deena and it didn't work out?

Spence wasn't about to let that happen. Alyssa had to come first. He owed that much to Evan.

God, please give me the strength to resist this woman. Spence stretched his arm to give Deena an arrow. "Give it another try."

It hurt to watch her draw that arrow back and not be standing behind her. But he made himself stand to the side and keep his arms folded as she shot arrow after arrow.

All of them hooked left.

twelve

After archery Deena and the girls headed to the commissary for lunch. As they neared the large log cabin, she spotted Pastor Rich sitting on one of the benches beneath the trees. His bald head slumped forward on his chest, and a low whistling noise originated from him.

"Quiet," Deena whispered as they drew closer to Pastor Rich. "The poor man needs some rest."

She was beginning to wonder how anyone made it through camp without collapsing from exhaustion. The campfire had lasted until past midnight, and then the girls had stayed up talking and laughing after everyone had gotten into bed.

"Aunt Deena, I just remembered. I left my water bottle back in the archery field. I'm going to need it this afternoon. Can I run back and get it?"

"Yes, but take a friend with you."

"I'll take Alyssa, if that's all right."

Deena smiled at the two girls. They seemed like unlikely friends—one tall and outgoing, the other small and quiet. She was pleased a bond seemed to be forming between them. "Okay," she said. "Meet us in the cafeteria. We'll be at our usual table."

It took Evie longer than it should have to return from the archery fields. Deena checked her watch and glanced across the crowded room to the door. No sign of Evie and Alyssa. She looked down at her half-eaten turkey sandwich and tried to reassure herself that nothing bad had happened. This was a church camp, and the girls knew where they were going. They were probably just enjoying a little independence. Still, when she checked her watch a few minutes later, she decided enough was enough. She headed for the door.

She didn't have to go very far before she saw them. The two girls were crouching beside the bench where Pastor Rich was napping. Deena headed toward them, wondering what they were doing bent over like that right next to Pastor Rich's feet.

Breaking into a jog, Deena closed the distance between herself and the girls. Glancing down, she felt her jaw drop in disbelief. Peeking out of the senior pastor's leather sandals were ten painted toenails. Evie held a bottle of hot pink polish in her hand, and Alyssa had neon blue.

Deena nudged Evie's shoulder. Her niece glanced up with an expression of pure mischief on her face. The little imp. Deena wanted to laugh but made herself frown instead.

Evie's lips folded in on themselves in an effort to bite back her laughter. Her shoulders shook so hard she could barely steady her hand enough to add a final dab of hot pink to Pastor Rich's pinkie toe. Nudging Alyssa, Evie capped her polish. As the two girls exchanged glances, a small note of laughter escaped Evie's mouth. Pastor Rich stirred on the bench.

The coconspirators raced back to the building. Deena stared down at the pastor's colorful toes. She wondered for one wild moment if she had time to find nail polish remover and return Pastor Rich's toenails to their natural state before he awakened. Of course she couldn't.

She squared her shoulders and touched Pastor Rich's shoulder. "I'm sorry," she blurted out the moment he opened his eyes. "Your toenails." She pointed at his feet.

Pastor Rich studied his brightly painted toes. He looked up a moment later, smiling. "Tell the girls I like the color. They did a good job."

"Aren't you upset?"

Pastor Rich shook his head. "I've been having a hard time pretending to be asleep for the past ten minutes. I could have stopped them, but they were having too much fun."

"Don't you want to talk to them? Give them a lecture about playing pranks?"

"No. They're not in trouble. Everything is fine, Deena. When I was a kid one summer at camp, I put shaving cream on all the windows of the senior pastor's cabin so he would wake up and think we had a freak snowstorm. What I really wanted, though, was his attention."

Deena frowned. Evie got lots of attention. It couldn't be that. But if Evie didn't want attention, just what did she want? She stared down at Pastor Rich's face. She thought she had never seen anyone so much at peace.

"How do you do it? Stay so calm?"

Pastor Rich chuckled. "I just remind myself that God is the One in control. He's the One who has the power and the purpose." He patted a space on the bench beside him. "Come sit with me for a moment."

Deena shook her head. "I'd like to, but the girls are inside. I'd better get back to them. You don't know whose toenails are in danger."

He studied her face a moment then smiled. "You're doing a good job, Deena, but don't forget you're not in this alone. If you need help, just ask for it."

"Thank you, Pastor Rich. I appreciate that."

thirteen

The call came in around one o'clock. The cabin counselor from the boys' blue cabin had scraped up his hand in a tug-of-war match in the mud pits. Would Spence mind coming over and taping it up?

It wasn't far to the big field. Spence cut through the archery fields, empty of campers now, skirted around the soccer fields and horseshoe pits, and then headed to the roped-off area that contained a huge mud pit. A group of boys and girls huddled beneath a makeshift shade structure. Spence headed toward them and felt his breath catch as he sighted the back of Deena's head. There was no mistaking the black, choppy layers of her hair and the square of her shoulders.

"Someone needed medical help?" Spence looked around the group.

A short man with a large bald spot and thick, black-rimmed glasses held his arm out. Even covered with mud, Spence recognized Mitt Collins. Yesterday morning Mitt had gotten a blister on his palm during his cabin's kayak lesson. As Spence treated it, Mitt had given him free tax advice.

"The tape you put on yesterday came off during the tug-of-war match," Mitt said with a note of apology in his voice. "I had to ask the referee to suspend the match until you could tape me up again."

Spence washed the wound and patted it dry with a gauze pad. It wasn't a deep blister, but it was in a painful place, located in the folds of his palm near the base of his thumb. "I can tape it up for you," he offered, "but I don't think you're going to be able to grip the tug-of-war rope very easily. And you really shouldn't let it get dirty."

The boys from Mitt's cabin groaned even as the girls

in Deena's cabin cheered.

"I don't want my boys to have to forfeit," Mitt said. "Is there anything you can do?"

Spence took some Coban and more gauze out of his bag. "Not really. You're probably going to make the blister worse if you try to grip the rope."

The boys groaned even louder. "We don't want to forfeit," one of them said. "We want to play."

A boy said, "Come on, Dad, please?"

Mitt looked at Spence. "Tell you what, Spence. You take my place in the match, and I'll do your taxes for free."

Spence squared his shoulders. He looked at the muddy field and the flag hanging from a line that marked the center of the pit. He glanced at Deena again and saw the challenge in her eyes. "You don't have to offer to do my taxes, Mitt," he said slowly, but loudly so everyone could hear him. "I'll do it for free."

The boys released a roar as if Spence had just announced they had qualified to play in the Super Bowl. They immediately began jumping up and down and bumping chests. Spence shot Deena a cocky grin. "If the blue girls' team finds no objection, that is."

"What do you say, girls?" Deena said. "Do you want to show these guys how to play tug-of-war?"

The girls responded with higher-pitched but no less enthusiastic shouts. Evie flexed her muscles, Lourdes grinned widely, Britty and Taylor gave each other high fives, and Alyssa gave Deena a big thumbs-up.

"Okay," Spence said. "It's settled."

"Thanks, Spence," Mitt said. "I owe you big-time. Lewis would have killed me if we'd had to forfeit."

"No problem," Spence said. "We're here to serve."

"One thing I ought to tell you. Be careful. Those girls. They're stronger than they look. The tall, black-haired gal, she could pull a stump out of the ground."

Spence laughed. "Thanks for the warning, Mitt, but we'll be fine."

The referee, a teenage boy wearing a mud-plastered T-shirt and shorts, gave a short blast on his whistle. "Everyone, take your positions on the field."

Deena walked with a very straight back into the mud. However, as she sank to her ankles, her shoulders came up and her elbows went out like wings. Her hips made an adorable little wiggle, and Spence thought he'd never seen anyone girlier in his entire life.

Releasing the grin he'd been holding back, Spence stepped into the mud after her. He had to admit, the muck had the consistency of quicksand. It sucked loudly at his feet as he picked his way to the starting point.

A dividing line hung across the middle of the field, and each team took one side. A red pennant hanging from the dividing line marked the middle of a fat, mud-stained rope.

The referee explained the rules and ordered them to take their places.

Spence organized his team by weight. He took the end position and put the heaviest kid, Zach, in front of him. He was just beginning to notice that all the kids on his team were pretty skinny. No problem. They could handle the girls.

On the other side of the centerline, the girl's team also arranged themselves by weight. He nearly laughed at Deena's expression of disgust as she gingerly picked up the mud-stained rope.

"Everyone ready?" the referee asked.

"Ready," Spence yelled, planting his feet in the slime.

"Ready," Deena echoed, hooking the rope behind her hips. She looked straight at him. "Bring it on."

The whistle blew, and the rope immediately went taut. Spence's strategy had been to hold back, letting Deena's team develop false confidence, and then drag them across the dividing line. However, as his team lost about six feet within seconds, Spence rapidly changed plans.

He leaned back and used every one of his 220 pounds to stop Deena's team from pulling them across the line. The maneuver halted their forward progress but didn't turn the tide in his favor.

To his surprise, the other team also increased their effort. Spence grunted and dug his heels into the slippery mud.

He glanced at Deena, red-faced, muscles straining, shouting encouragement to her team members. The woman might have the face of an angel, but Mitt had been right. She was as strong as an ox.

Inches in front of him, Zach leaned backward, nearly into his lap. "Pull!" Spence yelled.

His team was pulling for all they were worth, but they weren't moving. "Keep pulling," Spence roared, shifting as his feet slid forward an inch. His new strategy was simply to try to hold their position until Deena's team got tired. Then he'd reel them in like a fish on a line.

Suddenly Walter's feet flew out from under him. He fell backward into Lewis, who toppled backward into Brian, who knocked down Zach, and the next thing Spence knew, he was flat on his back. Cold mud rapidly worked its way up the legs of his shorts, and the finish line was only a few feet away.

Spence rolled onto his belly and struggled to get his legs in front of him. Unfortunately, his legs tangled up with Zach's. Before he knew it, the whistle blew.

"We have a winner!" the referee shouted. Deena's team cheered wildly. "But remember, it's a best of three match," the muddy teenager continued. "Contestants, switch sides and get ready for the next round."

Spence picked some mud from his ear. His clothing had collected about five pounds of wet mud. The rest of his team looked even worse. The girls were laughing at them and pumping their fists in the air in victory. Evie and Alyssa were bumping their hips together in a happy dance that stopped the second Alyssa saw him.

Spence felt more than the defeat of the tug-of-war match. Obviously bringing her to this camp had changed nothing. Maybe it was time he accepted she didn't want to live with him. Spence retreated. Six months ago his world had tilted, and since then it seemed everything he did was wrong.

The referee blew the whistle, signaling the start of the next round. Spence took his position at the end of the rope, and the irony was not lost on him. He was at the end of his rope. Clasping the thick, mud-coated rope, he welcomed the opportunity to vent a little frustration.

After the third game ended, Spence and his team slopped their way across the pit to shake hands with the members of Deena's team. In his entire life, he couldn't ever remember seeing a group of people so filthy looking.

There wasn't a patch of clean skin visible on anyone, but Spence had never seen any group of kids look so happy. He himself felt considerably better after thoroughly trouncing Deena's team.

He grinned as he came to a stop in front of Deena, whose red T-shirt was no longer recognizable as a shirt at all. It was a second skin of thick brown mud. The only spots of color on her were those blue eyes and red bow-shaped lips. His mood improved another notch.

"Congratulations," Deena said, offering her hand.

He grinned. "We got lucky. It was fun, wasn't it?"

She grinned back at him. "Yeah, but I think I have mud in my teeth."

"Me, too," Spence said, and it didn't bother him one bit. "You're pretty muddy." The words slipped out not the way he meant them at all. What he meant was she looked cute when she was muddy.

"You are, too," Deena said and flicked a bit of mud off her shoulder. It landed on Spence's shirt.

"Hey," he said and flicked some mud right back at her.

The next thing he knew, she shook her head, spraying him with hundreds of mud pellets. She was in trouble now. She knew it, too. Laughing, she turned and ran.

Only she couldn't quite run in the mud. Not very fast, anyway. He'd have her in two strides. Just what he intended to do with her when he caught her, he wasn't sure, but he was going to have fun finding out. He launched himself after her and quickly caught up. His arms had just barely managed to encircle her waist when his feet slipped out from under him.

They both went down, landing with a splash and the sound of cheers. He still had his arms around her, and she was shaking with laughter. He couldn't stop the idiotic grin that plastered itself across his face. Not when she smiled up at him like that.

The world had tilted again, but this time everything felt like it had fallen right into place.

fourteen

The beach ball smacked the concrete right next to her lounge chair. Deena reached out and swatted it back into the pool. A boy shouted his thanks, and the game of water polo continued.

Deena already had lost her iced tea to a shot that had gone wild, and twice the ball had whizzed just millimeters past her head. She was doing okay, though. Better than okay. She was actually having a lot of fun. She smiled. Spence tackling her in the mud had been really fun. In fact, she enjoyed just about anything they did together.

Darkness had not fully fallen yet, but the pool lights had come on, turning the water a fluorescent blue. A gentle breeze ruffled Deena's hair as she pondered a deep scientific question. What was Spence's best feature? He had great eyes, but that smile. . .it was killer.

She couldn't rule out his voice, either. It had that rumbly, deep pitch that made everything he said sound important. Well, almost everything. He had that sneaky sense of humor, too.

Deena flinched as another shot sailed over her head. A boy, dripping wet, vaulted out of the pool after it. She had to stop thinking so much about Spence, letting her imagination go wild. What if he was serious about her, and they ended up getting married? If she had a family, then she would have to be more like Stacy, making cookies and driving everyone to activities.

She'd have to worry about harsh teachers and inappropriate friends, body piercings, driver's ed, drugs, sex education, and. . . the list was endless.

Deena didn't see how she could be the kind of scientist she wanted to be and have a family, too. That meant there could be no more scientific thoughts about Spence.

An even louder roar arose from the pool, and then youthful bodies began clambering out of the water. Game over. Pizza and a movie came next. She'd better get moving if she wanted a slice of pepperoni.

She set her striped canvas tote on her seat and headed for the tables under the trees. Hurrying because a couple of days at camp had taught her there'd be no leftovers, she found her feet leading her in a different direction when she spied Evie by the drink cooler. She'd been wanting to speak to her niece privately, but up until now there just hadn't been an opportunity.

"Hi, Aunt Deena." Her niece wore a green one-piece Speedo with a towel wrapped around her waist. She had the beginnings of a suntan and looked quite lovely.

"I need to talk to you. About what you did to Pastor Rich's toenails." Deena pulled her off to the side.

Evie grinned. "I think he likes it. I saw him walking around, and the polish is still there."

"Evie, you can't go around playing pranks on people. Even though Pastor Rich wasn't mad, it's still not right."

Evie dropped her gaze to the ground. "Are you going to make me apologize to him?"

"Absolutely, and you and Alyssa both are going to offer to remove it for him. I sincerely doubt Pastor Rich brought nail polish remover to camp."

Evie shrugged. "Okay, Aunt Deena, but I have to tell you, I'm really disappointed. I thought you were a cool aunt."

Deena held Evie's gaze even though she couldn't help but feel slightly wounded. "I am a cool aunt," she said with more confidence than she felt. "Evie, these pranks, they aren't you. Don't get labeled a prankster. You're so much more than that."

Evie tugged her towel more tightly around herself. "Maybe you're wrong about who I am."

"I'm not wrong," Deena said. "You're a great kid."

Evie made a face as if being a great kid was a terrible thing.

"You are," Deena continued. "A great kid. Now how about

we get some pizza before it's all gone?"

They balanced plates with slices of pepperoni pizza and cans of soda and picked their way back to the pool area. The kids had spread out beach towels across the concrete deck and sat in small groups eating. Two counselors set up a large movie screen at the diving end of the pool. Evie spotted Alyssa sitting with Britty, Taylor, and Lourdes and stepped carefully around the bodies to join them.

Deena looked around for a spot to eat. She wanted to stay close to the pool so she could supervise the campers. She'd saved a spot with her beach bag, but the chair had been moved to make more space for the campers and their towels.

A nearby rock retaining wall seemed a good option. She wouldn't be able to see the movie very well, but it would be a nice place to eat. She had just taken her first bite of pizza when Spence walked up to her. "Want some company?"

"Sure." Her heart jumped a bit at the sight of him. She patted the top of the rock. "Just watch out. There are a few hungry ants crawling around."

Spence took his seat. "I can handle it." He bit into his pizza. "I take it you've recovered from the afternoon's activities."

"We clogged the drain in our shower getting all that mud off," Deena admitted. "I used the plunger, though, and everything went right down."

"I could look at it," Spence offered.

"Thanks, but it's under control." Which was more than could be said about her misbehaving heart thumping about in her chest like a wild thing in a cage. Her face burned, too, and she was pretty sure it had nothing to do with being in the sun. With effort, she took her gaze off his face. "You ever look at these kids and wonder what they'll do when they grow up?"

Spence laughed. "I'm still wondering what I'm going to do next." He finished his first slice of pizza and started on the second.

Deena remembered the study guide for the MCAT test on his desk. "You think you might want to be a doctor?"

Spence took his time answering. "I love being an EMT, but what I did isn't something that lends itself well to being a single dad. Not the kind of rescue I want to do."

"You mean you can't pull someone off a cliff and be home for dinner."

"More than that, I don't want Alyssa worrying all the time that something is going to happen to me."

The lights flickered on the movie screen, indicating the movie was about to begin. Neither Deena nor Spence made any move to sit where they could see the screen better.

"Well, you'll make a great doctor, if that's what you decide to do. Would you head into cardiology?"

"Maybe," Spence said, frowning, clearly unhappy with the question. "When you were a little girl, did you know you wanted to be a scientist?"

"I was never little," Deena said. "I was always tall. Every class picture, I'm in the back row." She hadn't liked being tall and would have much preferred to be average sized like Stacy. "I wasn't fat, but this girl in second grade just hated me. She always called me Diana the Giant."

"Your real name is Diana? How did you become Deena?"

Deena wiped her mouth with a napkin. "When I was sixteen I did this science fair project about DNA extraction from soil. I won first place, and afterward everyone starting calling me DNA—you know—deoxyribonucleic acid. Deena kind of stuck."

Spence set his empty plate aside. "Deena's a good name."

"Thanks. Spencer's a good name, too. Were you popular in high school?"

"That was my brother's gift. Wherever Evan went, the party started. I just tagged along."

"You're very likable, Spence." Quickly, before he took her words the wrong way, she added, "I mean, the kids in my cabin think you're really cool."

He looked away and stared into the shadows of the woods around them. "Tell that to Alyssa. Every time I get near her, she looks like she wishes the earth would open up and swallow her." He crumpled his can. "I don't know what I'm doing wrong."

"Maybe you're not doing anything wrong," Deena said gently. She thought about the fear Alyssa had expressed. The fear that she would forget her parents if she stopped grieving for them. "Give her more time."

"I don't have a lot of time," Spence snapped and then immediately apologized. "I'm sorry. You touched a sore spot. The only way I could get her to come to this camp was to promise her after the week ended she could choose between living with me and living with her grandparents in Texas."

Deena shifted on the rough surface of the wall. "She'll pick you. I'm sure of it."

"Then you haven't seen the way she looks at me. Our conversations aren't exactly deep and meaningful, either. The harder I try to show I care about her, the more it seems she hates me."

In the distance Deena could see the flickering images on the screen. The shapes of the kids were nothing more than dark lumps. She wondered which lump belonged to Alyssa.

"She doesn't hate you," Deena assured him. "She's a little confused about how she feels." Just like Deena had been— only instead of being angry at her father, she'd been furious with God for taking away her mother.

She remembered Rev. Moleman's long, sad face at her front door, valiantly explaining through the six-inch crack that God hadn't caused her mother's cancer. "If God doesn't change a circumstance, He will use it to His glory. He never wastes a tear, Diana."

She had practically slammed the door shut on him. But the irony of Spence's situation wasn't lost on her now. She could almost hear the old reverend whispering that the time had come when Deena's pain could be used as a blessing to others.

"My mom died, Spence, when I was sixteen. My sister, Stacy, was fourteen. My dad avoided me like the plague and couldn't get enough of Stacy. The only thing that seemed to please him about me was my report card. Otherwise, it seemed like he couldn't stand to be in the same room with me."

She didn't look at him. "I thought I'd done something wrong to make him dislike me so much. But one day when I walked into the room, he called me Evelyn by accident. I realized then why he couldn't bear to be with me. I look just like my mother. Before she got sick, that is."

"So what did you do?"

"I cut my hair." Deena looked past Spence at the still surface of the pool water. She remembered standing in front of the mirror in the upstairs bathroom and staring at herself. The scissors had felt so cold and heavy in her hands as she lifted them. Something in her had wanted to cry when the first hunk of long, wavy hair fell to the floor.

He was silent for a long moment. "Did it help?"

"Yeah," Deena said. "It did."

Spence touched her arm. "Deena, how did your mother die?"

Her mother's gaunt face, pale and exhausted, flashed through Deena's mind. She remembered the tears and the promises and the last time she'd kissed the warm curve of her mother's forehead.

"She had breast cancer," Deena said slowly. "She found a lump and had it biopsied. That led to her first mastectomy. Then they found another spot in her left breast, and she had another mastectomy. It didn't help, though. It kept coming back and coming back and coming back."

fifteen

Spence slid closer to Deena. He wanted to comfort her, put his arms around her, but was reluctant to do something others might misinterpret. He put his hand on her arm instead. "She'd be pretty proud of you, Deena. What you're doing with your life."

"I'm just telling you this because I think Alyssa isn't trying to push you away as much as she is trying to be loyal to her parents. When you showed up at the tug-of-war game this afternoon, I think she was pleased to see you. The rest was a big act."

As Spence struggled to process this information, Alyssa, Evie, Lourdes, Britty, and Taylor walked up to them.

"Movie is over," Evie informed him.

And it was. For the first time he realized the sound coming from the speakers had stopped and no images flickered on the large screen by the pool.

"We're tired," Evie said.

"And hungry," another girl said. He thought it might be Taylor, but in the moonlight he couldn't tell if her hair was red. He always got her mixed up with Britty.

"I'm a little cold," Lourdes said.

Deena responded immediately. "Oh, honey, let's get you my towel. It's in my bag. If I can find it."

"I think it's by the picnic tables," Spence said.

It didn't take much time to locate Deena's beach bag, but then Deena wanted to stay a little longer and help the other counselors put away the movie screen and stack deck chairs in the utility room. By the time they'd finished, it had grown dark. Spence borrowed a flashlight and volunteered to walk Deena and the girls back to their cabin.

He'd never minded being in the woods at night. Just the opposite. Sometimes when he couldn't quiet his mind, he liked to walk in the darkness. Or just sit outside and look up at the stars. He and God had had more than one conversation this way.

From the giggles and the way the girls had packed into tight clusters behind him, Spence realized they saw the darkness a totally different way.

"Did you hear that?" Evie asked.

"Hear what?" Lourdes said.

"That noise," Evie answered.

"Maybe it was my chewing gum," Taylor said. "I just popped a bubble."

Spence slowed, and Deena nearly walked right into his back. He shined the light at the girls' feet. "We're fine. Don't be scared."

One of the girls giggled. "Every time someone says that in a movie, someone ends up getting chased by another person carrying a very big knife."

"Britty," Deena said. "This isn't a movie. No one is going to come chasing us with a big knife."

Something rustled in the underbrush. Spence tried to listen, but the girls were making too much noise for him to tell. It was probably only an opossum, possibly a raccoon. He began walking again.

"It feels like we're in a cave," one of the girls said.

"Taylor, we're, like, climbing up a hill. How can it feel like we're in a tunnel?" Britty said.

"Because it's really dark," Lourdes replied.

"What if we got lost?" Taylor asked. "What would we do?"

"We're on the path," Spence assured her. "We're not going to get lost. But if you did get lost, the best thing to do is stay right where you are. I'll come find you. I promise."

"What about bears?" Taylor pressed. "Should we stay where we are if we get lost and a bear comes along?"

"Don't worry about bears," Spence said. "It's far more likely we'll run into a skunk. And even then, it wouldn't be a big deal. If you guys got sprayed, we'd mix up some hydrogen peroxide, baking soda, and dish soap, and it'd take the smell right out."

"I'd rather use my cucumber melon body spray," Britty said in a slightly smug tone. "It's got, like, neutralizing odor powers. That's what it says on the label."

"But if a bear jumped out from the woods, what should we do, Mr. Spence?" Taylor asked.

Deena half expected Britty would suggest spraying it with her Freeze and Shine hairspray, but nobody said anything, which told her the girls weren't entirely convinced they were safe.

"Just stand very still and let me handle it," Spence said. "I wouldn't let any of you get hurt."

They were silent for a moment, and then Britty stopped walking. "Did you hear that? I heard something. Branches cracking. Growling. I think something is stalking us!"

"You heard my stomach digesting," Deena said very firmly. "And we're almost at the cabin, right, Spence?"

"Very close," Spence agreed. "Sometimes noises can be misleading. Remember the night I slept on your porch? It was pretty late, and I was just about to go to sleep when I heard an animal growling. I thought it was a bear, but when I listened a little longer, I realized the noise was coming from *inside* the cabin." He paused. "And it wasn't an animal growling. It was someone snoring." He paused as the girls laughed. "One of you really knows how to cut wood."

There was silence; then Evie said soberly, "It was you, Aunt Deena."

Deena laughed. "Oh, Evie, I don't snore."

"You were snoring so loudly it sounded like airplanes taking off and landing," Spence said, thoroughly enjoying himself.

The girls giggled. "I'm sure you were dreaming about a wild animal growling," Deena replied.

He denied it, of course, and they bantered back and forth

until they reached the cabin steps. He paused as the girls said good night and ran inside. Of course Alyssa didn't pause to say anything to him, nothing at all, and the weight of disappointment settled over him.

Deena paused beneath the porch lights. Her dark hair gleamed, and he tried to imagine it long. Would it be straight or wavy? He wasn't sure. She would look beautiful either way. She also looked beautiful with short hair. It showed off the strength of her character, the bone structure that needed no enhancement.

"Thanks for walking us back," Deena said. "I hope you have good dreams. With no bears growling—or, rather, snoring."

"If I were dreaming," he said for her ears only as he stared straight at her, "I could think of a lot better things than a bear snoring." He locked gazes with her so she'd know exactly what he meant. "Night, Diana. Sleep well."

She stiffened. "Please, Spence, call me Deena. It's who I am now."

"Okay, Dee," he teased. "See you in the morning."

She made an exasperated noise, shook her head, and smiled as if she couldn't help herself. "Good night, funny guy. Try to take the night off from rescuing someone, okay?" The screen door creaked as she pulled it open and then lightly banged shut behind her.

sixteen

Her alarm clock went off. Deena stirred. It felt like she'd just gone to bed. It couldn't be time to get up already. She opened her eyes and tried to focus. Everything looked a bit blurry. The ceiling looked different. Lower. A lot lower. Like inches above her face. And made out of a white, gauzy material.

She blinked and lifted her fingers to explore. Something as soft as Kleenex was wrapped all around her. Then it hit her what had happened. Someone had rolled her bed in toilet paper.

"Evie!"

A chorus of giggles split the silence.

Deena ripped a hole in the covering and sat up. Her entire bunk had been rolled, and streamers of loose toilet paper hung over the edges. From below five girls laughed up at her.

"This isn't funny," Deena said. She pulled a length of tissue from her hair. "Evie?"

"I'm sorry," Evie said, sounding anything but. "But last night you were snoring, just like Mr. Spence said, and none of us could sleep. So we decided to play a joke on you."

"What if I'd suffocated?"

"We left you air holes. Did you know, Aunt Deena, that you're a really sound sleeper? One of the rolls got dropped on your head, and you didn't even wake up."

Deena shook her head. How many times did she have to make excuses for Evie? Why couldn't a girl as intelligent as her niece understand that pranks weren't funny?

"Are you mad at us?" This came from Britty, who was twisting a length of her blond hair around her finger. Taylor, chewing her usual wad of gum, looked a little worried, too.

Deena climbed down from the bunk. "No. Not mad. But

90

I am disappointed. Please clean this mess up while I figure out what I'm going to do about this." She marched off in the direction of the bathroom.

"Aunt Deena?"

"Yes, Evie?"

"Are you going to tell my mother about this?"

It was the last thing Deena wanted to do. Stacy needed to rest. She studied the girl's face as another thought suddenly occurred to her. "Do you want me to tell her? Is that why you keep doing things like this?"

Evie laughed. "Of course not. I absolutely do not want you to tell my mother."

"You sure?" What, then? What was reinforcing Evie's behavior? Deena took another step toward the bathroom.

"You might not want to go in there," Evie warned.

"Why?" The hair on the back of Deena's neck stood up. "Why wouldn't I want to go in there?"

"Because," Evie said, trying unsuccessfully not to giggle, "we're out of toilet paper."

❧

They very nearly missed breakfast. By the time they'd gone through the cafeteria lines, the room was nearly empty. All except for Pastor Rich, who was just finishing a cup of coffee. He waved at her, and Deena wondered why he wasn't already at the amphitheater, preparing for the morning service.

Only on closer inspection, she realized it wasn't Pastor Rich at all.

Deena slid into a seat across from Spence. "You shaved your head." She set her tray down on a cafeteria table. "For a moment I thought you were Pastor Rich."

"I didn't shave my head," Spence protested. "I cut it short. Only it came out slightly shorter than I thought it would."

Deena tried not to stare. He'd pretty much scalped himself. She had to admit, though, that he looked almost as good in the buzz cut as he did with longer hair. "I like it."

Spence looked unsure. "You sure?"

Deena grinned. "Yeah, I do."

"The main thing is, do I look different?"

"You look very different," Deena assured him. "I hardly recognized you at first."

"Good."

"Hey, Mr. Spence," Evie said, joining them at the table. "You look like a soldier. One of those special agent guys." She and the rest of the girls from their cabin took seats around them.

"I'm still just a camp nurse," Spence replied, but his gaze traveled to his niece and stayed there. "What do you think, Alyssa?"

The girl took her time pouring maple syrup on her french toast and didn't look up. "I think you look like Pastor Rich."

Deena very nearly laughed and managed only by extreme effort to shoot Spence a sympathetic look. "She means you look very pastorish, very spiritual."

"My head is not shaved." Spence bent his head so they could examine it. "It must be the lighting in here."

"Must be the lighting," Deena agreed, and the girls laughed— all but Alyssa.

Unfortunately, Spence noticed this as well. It nearly broke Deena's heart to see the disappointment in his eyes. Obviously he'd taken the story she'd told him last night to heart. He had changed his appearance so there was no chance Alyssa would think Spence looked like his brother. However, while cutting her hair had helped her father to see Deena in a new way, it obviously wasn't working for Spence.

"What do you think, Alyssa?" Deena tried. "Do you think he'd look better with a Mohawk?"

"No. Uncle Spence looked better before." She turned to Evie. "You want my bacon?"

Spence looked at Deena, who shrugged. *Keep trying,* she wanted to whisper. Even if Alyssa didn't understand, she did.

"Be careful," Deena warned as Evie popped the entire strip into her mouth. "I nearly broke a tooth trying to chew that bacon."

"Oh, Aunt Deena," Evie said, speaking through a full mouth. "Didn't anyone tell you that you have to let it soak in your mouth for a little bit?"

Deena laughed. "No, they didn't, but I learned the trick to eating the cold eggs." She grinned. "You hold your nose when you eat them." She glanced around. No one was laughing.

"TMI." Britty shook her blond head.

"Too much information," Taylor translated.

"Your eggs wouldn't have been cold if you hadn't been so late to breakfast," Spence pointed out.

"We would have been here earlier if we hadn't had to hike to the pool cabana for extra supplies." She stared pointedly at Evie.

"We wrapped Aunt Deena in toilet paper," Evie reported happily. "I mean her bunk. When she was in it."

Spence set down his coffee cup. "You what?"

Deena nodded. "It was like waking up in a Kleenex box."

The girls exchanged looks and giggled. All but Alyssa, who pushed her french toast around her plate.

"I've never woken up in a Kleenex box," Spence said. "But one Halloween I had my brother, Evan, wrap me in toilet paper. I was supposed to be a mummy. Evan wound me so tight I couldn't bend my legs, and I couldn't climb the front steps to any of the houses when we trick-or-treated. Terrible idea. He didn't share his candy."

Alyssa stood abruptly. "Excuse me, but I need to use the bathroom."

Deena frowned and rose to her feet, only to find Evie already in motion. "I'll go," she said.

The other girls rose as well. They disappeared en masse in the direction Alyssa had gone, leaving Deena alone with Spence.

"Girls like to go in groups to the restroom," Deena said, but she hated to see Spence look so discouraged.

"The restrooms are in the other direction," Spence said. "I shouldn't have mentioned Evan."

He looked so upset that Deena wanted to wipe away the lines of worry etched across his face. "You didn't say anything wrong. Someday she's going to cherish hearing about your memories of her father."

"Not all of them." Spence crumpled his empty paper cup. "Not all of them."

❧

Deena slipped into the back of the amphitheater just as the morning service began.

Several rows down, she spotted Evie's copper hair. She and Lourdes had sandwiched Alyssa, with Britty and Taylor making bookends.

The worship music began. She was getting used to the volume of it, and although her teeth began to vibrate, she couldn't help tapping her foot to the beat of the music.

Her mother would have loved this camp. She would have volunteered, too, if her health had permitted. It was easy to imagine her now, singing along in that off-key voice that Deena would give anything to hear again.

Other memories stirred. Her mother bragging to other people that Deena had read the warning label on the Pampers box before she'd been old enough to be out of diapers. Her mother telling Deena that her intelligence was a gift from God and someday she would have an opportunity to use her gift for His glory.

Deena looked across the lake. She had tried so hard to keep her promise to her mother, to help others with breast cancer. Yet sometimes she felt so empty and lonely on the inside that she wasn't sure she could even make it through another day.

The music ended, and Pastor Rich spoke into the microphone. "Good morning, Camp Bald Eagle!"

"Good morning, Pastor Rich!" the campers roared.

"I can't hear you!" Pastor Rich teased, his bald head glistening in the sunlight.

"Good morning, Pastor Rich!"

Not only could Pastor Rich hear that, but so could anyone within ten miles.

"What day is this?"

The kids yelled, "It's Luau Day!"

Deena groaned. She'd been dreading this part of the camp ever since she'd read about it in the cabin counselor's training guide. Everyone was supposed to dress in grass skirts and wear leis. And if that weren't ridiculous enough, that evening every cabin would put on a skit in front of the entire camp.

"It's Luau Day," Pastor Rich confirmed. "And we're going to have some fun!"

The kids cheered wildly.

"We're going to have a pig roast and a talent show tonight," Pastor Rich said. "Each cabin will provide us with a skit. It can be musical, or lyrical, or anything you choose, but it must have a Hawaiian theme. We'll have some materials available in the commissary that you can use. All of you"—here he paused to open his arms to indicate everyone in the audience—"will be voting on the skits, and the winners will get to ride on the lake on a banana boat during the last day of camp."

A banana boat? Deena didn't even know what a banana boat was. As far as she was concerned, someone else could enjoy an afternoon on the lake riding a piece of fruit. She wasn't dressing up like an island girl or as anything else. She hadn't worn a costume in twenty-five years, and even then it had been Halloween.

"You will be judged on creativity, props, and story line," Pastor Rich continued. "Good luck, and aloha!"

Aloha? Everyone else could prance around in a grass skirt, but Deena definitely was sitting this one out.

seventeen

Deena smoothed the strands of her crinkly grass skirt. If any of her fellow researchers saw her now, they would never let her live it down. She still couldn't believe the girls had talked her into performing with them. She wasn't a hula dancer. She was a scientist. Scientists wore lab coats, not grass skirts, plastic leis, and ridiculous pink plastic hibiscus flowers in their hair.

"Girls' blue cabin, you're on deck. Are you ready?"

Deena stared at the perky young counselor holding the clipboard. Yes, she was ready. Ready to check herself into the nearest psychiatric facility. "Yes, we're all here."

In just a few moments, she and the girls would step out onto the amphitheater stage.

Mr. Crackers shifted on her shoulder, and she winced at the feel of his claws on her skin. *It's all your fault*, she wanted to tell the bird. If only Evie hadn't thought including the parrot in their skit would add authenticity, Deena would be in the audience, maybe even enjoying the show.

Behind her Britty asked, "Does anyone have a safety pin? My skirt is, like, a little big."

And Deena's was a little small. That was the problem with one-size-fits-all grass skirts. "I thought we pinned your skirt, Britty, honey."

"We did, but the safety pin, like, must have fallen off when we walked over here."

"Tuck it into the waistband of your shorts," Deena advised.

Polite applause greeted the team currently performing onstage. Deena shifted her weight.

From the stage, two boys began talking. Their dialogue seemed to consist of two words and two words only: "Unga munga." However, each used different inflections and emphasis.

It was silly, but kind of funny, too. Judging by the laughter coming from the spectators, they thought so, too.

"I feel sick," Taylor announced. "I may throw up."

"It's just stage nerves," Deena assured her. "Did you finish that peppermint Life Saver I gave you?"

"Yes," Taylor said sadly. "You don't have another, do you?"

"No."

"Unga munga!"

"Oh. Unga munga munga!"

"What are they saying?" Lourdes asked. "I don't understand a word."

"They aren't speaking English." Deena added, "You really look lovely, Lourdes, with your hair all loose like that."

" 'Lyssa," Evie said. "Take off your glasses."

"But I can't see without them."

"You don't need to see," Evie pointed out. "You just need to do everything we've been practicing all day. Besides, hula dancers don't wear glasses."

"Where will I put them?"

"Stick them in your coconuts," Britty advised, adjusting her own set.

Despite the coolness of the evening, Deena's forehead broke out in sweat.

"Are you ready?" Pastor Rich asked then swung back the sheet.

Deena drew a shaky breath and walked onto the stage. The spotlight nearly blinded her. The audience looked like one big blur of darkness. Around her the girls scurried about, setting out the cardboard palm trees that listed just as badly as Jeff's tree house.

"Ladies and gentleman," the announcer boomed. "I now have the pleasure of introducing our next performers. Please join me in welcoming the girls' blue cabin!"

Polite applause greeted them. Deena took her place and arranged her arms in the same position she'd seen in the Internet photo of a hula dancer.

Their music, also downloaded from the Internet, started. On the fifth note, just as they'd practiced, they all started to hula.

Deena tried not to wiggle around too much. If Mr. Crackers gripped her shoulder any more tightly, it was going to take a surgical procedure to get him off.

Lourdes, who had been miked, began to narrate their skit. Her sweet voice easily carried up the hill. "We are all hunters looking for that next big trophy to hang on the wall of our lives."

This was the cue for the girls to move around the stage fluttering their arms and hunting each other among the cardboard palms.

"Every waking moment of every day we think about that next trophy, imagining it will bring us happiness."

Alyssa walked into one of the cardboard palm trees, which immediately fell over.

"We hunt popularity," Lourdes said. "But that isn't enough. We hunt good grades, but still it doesn't fill the void inside. We hunt the mall for the right clothes, for iPods, MP3 players, cell phones, and computers. And still we're restless, hunting, thinking about what we want. What we need. The next thing that will make us happy."

Britty's skirt was hanging precariously low, and Deena reached out and hiked it back up as the blond danced past.

"But what we're looking for, what we really want, isn't something you buy. You can't find it at the mall, or save up for it with your allowance, or get it from your friends. We're looking for a relationship with the God who made us. He is the only One who can fill us with His everlasting love."

All the girls lifted their arms, and Taylor and Britty, who had taken tumbling classes together in fourth grade, did simultaneous backflips then went straight into splits.

Deena beamed as the audience enthusiastically clapped and whistled. Their show wasn't over; there still was one more part of their skit. The audience needed to be quiet before they could do it, so they all had to stand there for a while. It was hard to maintain a big smile for such a long period of time, but finally all the cheers subsided and the applauding become more sporadic and then stopped entirely. Finally, the amphitheater fell quiet.

It was time for the grand finale. Deena stepped forward into the spotlight. She looked at Evie to cue the parrot to say, "Aloha!"

Her niece coughed.

The bird stretched his wings and squawked loudly, "P-U. Who cut the cheese?"

Deena felt her jaw drop. *Please tell me Mr. Crackers didn't just say that. Not here. Not now.*

Evie coughed again.

"P-U," Mr. Crackers shouted happily. "Who cut the cheese?"

The audience started to laugh. Deena glanced around. Evie was holding her nose and trying not to laugh.

Evie.

Deena felt her blood start to boil. How could she? She must have been planning this for some time. Deena turned toward her, more upset than she had been in a long time. Maybe even in her entire life. So what if the audience was laughing and applauding like crazy. Her niece had done it again, played a prank when Deena had specifically asked her to stop. And this time she'd used poor Mr. Crackers.

The poor bird, however, seemed to be enjoying his moment in the spotlight. "P-U," he squawked as the audience whistled and shouted. "Who—"

"Aloha!" Deena shouted over the bird's voice. She marched toward the side exit with Mr. Crackers clinging to her shoulder like a bird caught in a strong gale wind. She stepped behind the sheet separating the backstage area and realized the rest of the girls weren't following. She pulled the sheet back.

The girls were still onstage. Evie, the little monkey, was waving her hand around as if she were trying to clear the air. Lourdes had doubled over, and Britty and Taylor clung to each other, laughing so hard they no longer could produce any sound.

And Alyssa. Deena blinked. The girl's head was thrown back and her ponytail bounced with the force of her laughter. She was transformed—so beautiful it almost took her breath away.

This was the Alyssa Spence had known existed deep inside but could not reach. Deena couldn't breathe. She just stared at the girl who had once been Allergy Girl and saw the transforming delight on her face.

"Girls!" Deena whispered loudly. "Come here!"

With final bows to the audience, the girls moved in Deena's direction. As they slipped through the gap in the sheet, they hugged each other, limp from laughter but sparkly-eyed with success.

Deena stared at their flushed faces, wondering if she should be strict or soft and feeling incredibly stupid because she was thirty-five years old and had no idea whether she should punish Evie or thank her.

"Come on, ladies," she said, stalling and also trying to find a more private area to talk to them. The sandy part of the beach provided her solution. "That was an awesome performance," she said as they gathered around her. "Now drop down and give me twenty."

Evie stared at her with eyes as bright as stars. "Twenty what?"

"Push-ups," Deena stated firmly. "You crossed the line by teaching Mr. Crackers an inappropriate phrase. Do you know how hard it's going to be to train him not to say that whenever someone coughs?"

"I'm sorry," Evie said. "I take total responsibility. It was my idea. The punishment should be mine and mine alone." Her chin, small and slightly pointed, tilted skyward.

"No," Alyssa said firmly. "It wasn't just you. I helped." She dropped to the sand.

"So did I." Britty joined Alyssa on the sand.

A moment later all the girls were lying facedown struggling

with the push-ups. None of them could actually do a push-up, but they were trying, giggling and gasping encouragement to each other.

Somehow, somewhere along the way, they'd bonded—become more than five girls who shared the blue cabin.

They'd become friends.

eighteen

Spence pushed his way through the laughing crowd. He glimpsed Deena heading toward the water. He picked up the pace, nearly colliding with a boy holding a huge cardboard sailfish.

"Sorry," he mumbled, steadying the boy.

Stepping beyond the perimeter of the amphitheater, he scanned the semidarkness. What had just happened? The dance had been cute and Lourdes's narration moving. Just seeing Deena in that grass skirt had been hugely entertaining. And then the grand finale.

Who had taught that bird that phrase? Not Deena—he'd seen the shock on her face. But it really didn't matter who. He'd seen Alyssa's face. It was the face of a girl having the time of her life.

He scanned the beach area for a group. The area seemed deserted; then he spotted a tall shape near the water. He moved closer.

He saw Deena illuminated in the moonlight. She had her hands on her hips and was studying five dark shapes in the sand. He paused. The kids were doing. . .push-ups?

"Deena!"

She looked up. "Hey, Spence."

"What's going on?"

"Push-ups."

"I can see that." He reached her side. "Why?"

"Because of the prank," Deena said matter-of-factly as if he should know. "You think Mr. Crackers was supposed to ask who cut the cheese?"

"Ten," Evie shouted breathlessly. "That's ten."

"It was funny," Spence said.

"It was inappropriate. I just hope none of us gets kicked out of camp."

Spence touched her arm. The feel of her skin did things to him on the inside that he prayed didn't show on the outside. "I've never heard of anyone getting kicked out of church camp."

"We could be the first," Deena said. "Stacy warned me. She said to always be prepared for the worst. 'Stay on your toes, Deena; you can't control teenagers like you can your lab experiments. Think chaos theory.' She was right."

"Fifteen," Evie groaned. "Can we stop now?"

"No," Deena said.

"It's okay, Deena. Even Pastor Rich was laughing. Don't make more of this than it is."

"I'm not, but if I don't do something, Spence, the next time it might be something even worse. I've been much too lackadaisical about this whole pseudoparenting thing."

More groans emanated from the girls. One of them collapsed on her belly and just lay there. His gaze traveled to Alyssa illuminated in the moonlight. For a moment, he imagined it was Evan lying there struggling to meet their dad's punishment.

How many times had he and Evan lain in that same position doing push-ups until it felt like their arms were on fire and their bodies weighed a million pounds? It'd been torture then, but looking back he realized he had never felt closer to his older brother than when they were both grunting in pain and exhaustion.

He missed Evan.

He dug the tip of his sneaker into the sand. He'd let his brother down so badly. He should have seen beneath the happy-go-lucky smile and slap on the shoulder. But no, Spence had been so busy saving total strangers that he'd failed to see his brother needed him even more.

Worse than failed to see. If he was brutally honest, he'd admit he'd known something was wrong with Evan. Maybe not 100 percent certain, but he'd silenced the voice that said the drink in his brother's hand was there far too often. He hadn't wanted to know. That was the truth that kept him up at night.

He would not make that mistake again. God came first, of course, but family came second. And the best way to make up for his failure to his brother was to care for Alyssa. Best he could, he'd raise her right.

"Twenty!" Evie shouted.

Twenty had come pretty fast on the heels of fifteen, but Spence kept that thought to himself. The girls scrambled to their feet, laughing and shaking sand from their clothing and limbs.

"Can we go back to the amphitheater and watch the rest of the performances now?" Evie asked.

"Sure," Deena replied. "Save me a seat. I'll be with you in a minute." Her gaze traveled to his face, and the look said she wanted to be alone with him. Despite the orders of his brain, his heart picked up its beat.

As soon as the girls were out of earshot, Deena turned to him, grinning. "Did you see Alyssa's face when Mr. Crackers spoke? It was like looking at another girl. I didn't know she could be like that."

"She hasn't been like that for a long time," Spence said. "Thank you, Deena. I had my doubts, but you're reaching her in a way I never could have."

Deena waved off his praise. "If you're going to give anyone credit, you probably need to give it to my wild niece." She shook her head, loosening the pink hibiscus pinned just above her ear. "Every time she opens her mouth, I'm terrified what's going to come out of it."

"She's good hearted, like her aunt." Spence's fingers itched to straighten that hibiscus, and not because he cared it was drooping. He simply wanted to touch her. "By the way, where'd you learn to hula like that?"

"Oh, the Internet. You should have seen the girls practicing,

Spence. Every one of us heard a different beat. And the hip movements. The instructions said to move from our knees, but none of us could get it until Britty told us to pretend we were putting on the world's tightest jeans."

He would have paid money to see that. He realized then that he didn't want to miss anything else. Not this week, and not beyond that. Here in the moonlight, his heart couldn't make it any clearer that this woman belonged with him. With him and Alyssa.

"Let's take a walk," he said.

"I probably should get back," Deena said, glancing back at the brightly lit amphitheater.

"The girls will be fine for a few minutes." He reached for her hand. "Please. It's such a nice night."

Deena hesitated. "What about Mr. Crackers?"

"He can come, too. We're not going far. There's just something I want to show you."

She hesitated a second time and again glanced at the amphitheater. "Maybe just a short one, but then I have to get back."

The shoreline quickly changed from sandy to rocky. Spence moved slowly, giving Deena time to pick her way over the uneven surface. The water lapped softly, a gentle, soothing noise that came out of the darkness, almost lost in the night. They followed the shoreline, and it wasn't long before they reached the boathouse and the long arm of the dock reaching out into the lake.

"This is where I wanted to bring you," Spence said, stepping up onto the wooden platform. "It's really beautiful out here at night."

Their footsteps sounded hollow as they walked out on the dock. It was a clear night, and the stars shone down on them. "This is beautiful," Deena whispered. "It's almost like we're standing on moonlight."

You're beautiful, he thought. *Inside and out*. He had always calculated the risk in getting involved in a relationship, but standing next to her, he felt like throwing caution to the wind. He had to clench his hands into fists to keep from reaching for her. This wasn't just a summer camp fling, he realized. His feelings went deeper, well beyond that. Spence closed his eyes.

He saw the irony of the whole situation. He had built a career based on rescuing people. Finding them when they were lost and patching them up when they hurt themselves. He'd come to this camp, in fact, with the hope that it would allow him to rescue his niece emotionally and spiritually. He had been so sure her healing would begin here.

It had never occurred to him, though, that the person who needed rescuing most just might be himself.

And Deena might very well be the only woman who could do it.

nineteen

"I still can't believe we won the skit competition," Lourdes remarked as they headed for the stable area the next morning.

"It's going to be so cool going out on that banana boat," Evie exclaimed. "I can't wait!"

Deena had nearly been struck dumb when Pastor Rich had announced their cabin as the winner, but it had been a crazy night. Seeing Alyssa come out of herself. Taking that walk with Spence. There was something special about this camp. Stacy had been right. It was life changing.

Taylor popped a bubble. "You were right, Evie. Mr. Crackers was our secret weapon."

Deena frowned. "We were fortunate that no one was offended by what Mr. Crackers said. Absolutely no more pranks. Got it, girls?" She gave Evie a sideways glance.

"No more pranks, Aunt Deena." Evie's voice was pure innocence.

"No more pranks," Taylor, Britty, Lourdes, and Alyssa chimed in, but they giggled.

Now that she had been in charge of the girls for almost a week, Deena had a whole new respect for Stacy. Parenting required all sorts of skills—medical, psychological, athletic, even creative ones like dancing and acting. It was all very exhausting. But fun, too.

They reached the big red barn. The horses were already saddled and tied to a hitching post outside the stable. Deena's steps slowed. The only animal she was used to being around was Mr. Crackers, and he was a lot smaller than these horses. She swallowed. Why couldn't the girls simply play horseshoes this morning? Did they absolutely have to go riding?

A teenage girl stepped out of the barn. She had on jeans

and a pair of chocolate-colored chaps. "Good morning," she said. "Let's get you all some safety helmets to wear; then I'll assign you each a horse to ride."

A few minutes later, Deena tugged the strap of her helmet unhappily. "Are you sure this one is gentle?" she asked. The equine giant in front of her kept tossing its huge head up and down. The horse's feet were enormous, too—like dinner plates.

"Petunia is very gentle," Kendra, the riding instructor, assured her. Of course Kendra, like most of the counselors in the camp, looked about fifteen years old. Kids that age didn't understand that when you were older than thirty, you started thinking about things like breaking your neck.

"It's chewing that bit like it wishes it were my arm," Deena pointed out.

"Don't worry," Kendra said.

Deena hesitated. The last horse she'd ridden had been on the carousel at the mall. She'd gotten kind of woozy after the second time it went around. "Isn't there a smaller horse?"

Kendra, who barely reached Deena's shoulder, was putting all her ninety or so pounds into tightening the girth. Even Deena, who knew absolutely nothing about horses, could tell the beast was holding its breath. They hadn't given her a dumb one, and this realization wasn't helping with her anxiety.

She wondered if horses, like dogs, could smell fear. She patted its hairy neck tentatively, and the horse twitched as if she'd tickled it with a feather. It rolled one huge brown eye back at her and chomped enthusiastically on the metal bit.

Kendra kneed the horse in its stomach and jerked the girth tight. Sweating, she wiped her forehead and motioned for Deena to climb aboard.

Get on now? The horse was probably angry about just having been kneed in the stomach.

There it went again, chewing on the bit and shivering as if it had something crawling beneath its skin. "Why's he doing that? I mean she."

"Petunia is just shooing flies." The teenager moved to the opposite side of the horse and leaned against the other stirrup. "You can get on now."

Yeah, right. The horse seemed tall as a mountain. Deena drew a deep breath then tried to put her foot in the stirrup. It was a bit of a stretch, so she dropped the reins and wrapped her hand around the pommel of the saddle. She leaned back a little and managed to hook the stirrup.

This accomplished, she paused to rest for a minute, and as she did, two horses walked past in single file. Without any warning, Deena's horse fell into step behind them. Deena, attached by the stirrup, had to hop alongside. She sailed right past Britty, who was in the process of adjusting her stirrups.

"Miss Deena, what are you doing?" Britty's voice rang with horror.

Deena didn't have the breath to reply. Petunia seemed to be picking up speed, and she had to use all her energy to hop along beside her. Deena had no idea how long she could keep this up, but then, fortunately, the horse in front of them stopped. Petunia, either dumber than Deena had thought or exceptionally nearsighted, bumped into the other horse's rear and stopped.

Panting, Deena tried to pull her foot free of the stirrup. No success—her left foot remained firmly wedged in the wooden triangle.

"I thought you had her," Kendra, seconds behind, snapped. "You were supposed to hold the reins."

With her legs still locked in a near split stretch, Deena did not feel in the position to argue. "Sorry."

She waited until Kendra had a grip on both the horse and the saddle, then muscled her way into the saddle. Once aboard, she realized the world had taken on a new splendor.

"Hold your reins like this," Kendra instructed. Deena barely heard her. She kept looking around, awed by how different everything looked from the back of a horse.

The transformation was amazing. Thrilling, even. Like the

first time she'd peered through a microscope and watched a whole new world come into focus.

If someone had told her a week ago she would be horseback riding in the foothills of the Berkshires, she would have laughed them out of her laboratory.

But now she could see Stacy had been right—there was a whole world beyond her laboratory that she knew nothing about. She took a deep breath. Well, she was discovering it now. And she liked it.

She wished Spence was there to see her being adventurous. Successfully adventurous. Not falling into a patch of poison ivy, getting clunked on the head with a kayak paddle, or hitting other people's targets on the archery field.

The line moved forward, each horse following the one in front through a wooden gate and into a grassy field. A thin brown line marked the path, and on each side lush green grass grew as high as the horses' knees. A cool, gentle breeze riffled the strands of Deena's hair, and the sunshine felt strong and warm on her face.

The rocking motion of the horse lulled her. She allowed herself to relive last night's moonlit walk with Spence. Standing on the dock with him had been the most romantic moment she'd ever experienced.

The reins slipped through her fingers as Petunia put her head down to graze. The mare's strong jaws ripped off a good-sized chunk of grass. Deena tried to pull the horse's head up, but it would have been easier to lift a block of concrete.

"Give her a kick," Kendra yelled from atop the lead horse.

Deena tapped the horse's sides tentatively with her heels. The horse didn't move.

"Harder," Kendra yelled.

Deena nudged Petunia's sides a bit harder. She didn't want to hurt her. She strained to pull up the horse's head, which now seemed firmly bolted to the ground. Nobody else's horse seemed so hungry. Petunia tore at that grass like a power mower.

Deena peered down the long slide of the mare's neck. She didn't see how the horse could chew with that metal bit in its mouth. What if Petunia started choking? Did you give a horse the Heimlich?

Petunia now had a substantial wad of grass sticking out of her mouth. Deena was about to point this out to Kendra, but then the horse went into a convulsion. Every inch shivered violently.

Deena's feet flew out of the stirrups. She had a last, awful thought that they'd given her a horse with mad cow disease; then the world turned upside down. The next thing she knew, she was lying flat on her back in the grass.

twenty

Spence was getting ice for a boy who had bitten his lip on the Leap of Faith when Deena limped into his clinic. She waved feebly and sank into one of the waiting chairs.

He instructed the boy to ice his lip for fifteen minutes, patted his bony shoulder, and told him to be more careful next time. The boy had hardly made it through the door, when Spence hurried over to Deena.

She seemed okay—there was grass in her hair and a small dirt stain on her jeans. "Deena, what happened?"

She smiled. "I hurt my toe. It's nothing, really. I wouldn't have bothered you, but the girls insisted."

"Let's take a look." He put his arm around her. Leaning most of her weight against him, he walked her to the examination table.

"Spence, I can walk. You really don't have to—"

"Shh. Just tell me what happened." He helped her onto the exam table and reached for her sneaker.

"I fell off a horse," Deena admitted.

He checked her eyes for signs of a concussion. Thankfully her pupils looked fine, and Spence relaxed a little. "You fell off a horse and landed on your toe?"

"No. That happened afterward."

Spence pulled off her white cotton sock and saw the problem immediately. Her big toe was swollen and an angry red color.

"Can you move it?" He tested the joint, and when he was satisfied it wasn't broken, he set her foot down and retrieved an ice pack from the mini refrigerator.

"Yeah, but it hurts. Spence, the horse had an agenda."

Horses didn't have agendas, and he had to hide a smile at

the notion. "And you think this because. . . ?"

"It pretended to be dumb, but it wasn't." Deena stiffened as he placed the ice pack on her injured toe. "It pulled the reins out of my hands and started eating grass. When I peeked to see if it was choking, it started shaking wildly, throwing me off. And then when I got to my feet, it stepped on my toe and wouldn't get off. I pushed and pushed. This was not a thin horse, Spence."

He was going to laugh. If he as much looked at her face, it was all over. He bit his lip. "I don't think your toe is broken," he managed. "You just need some ice and some ibuprofen."

"You think it's funny." She looked wounded.

He swallowed. "No, I don't. It had to be very frightening. And painful." And funny. He wanted to laugh so badly it hurt.

"I'm not much of a nature girl, huh?"

No, she wasn't. She looked so cute sitting there, all blue eyed and rumple haired. It was all he could do not to pull her into his arms. Instead, he pulled a blade of grass from her hair. "You don't have to be an outdoors girl. I like you just the way you are."

She looked away. "Maybe you just don't know me." It was almost a mumble and the last thing he would expect her to say. The small showing of insecurity gave him the impetus to plunge forward.

"Listen, I've been thinking. What do you say I take you out when this camp ends?"

"Out?" She paused. "Out where?"

"Anywhere you want."

"You mean go out on a date?" Her light blue eyes found his. The fear in them wasn't flattering. Still, he'd come this far, and there was no retreating.

"Yeah. Dinner and a movie."

Silence.

"You can pick the movie." He heard the tension in his voice but couldn't seem to do anything about it. "I prefer an action type, but I'm open to one of those chick flicks, too."

Deena studied the speckled tile floor. A very bad feeling took root in his stomach. "You're involved with someone, aren't you?" Idiot. He should have guessed.

"No, it's not that."

"Then what?"

"It's my job, Spence. I practically live in my lab. I don't have time for a personal life." She shifted higher on the exam table. "But thanks for asking."

He should let it go. Question asked and answered. Anything further bordered on harassment. Yet as he looked at her, she seemed more in pain than when she'd limped into his clinic. He leaned forward. "We can forget the movie, then, but how about the dinner? Even cancer researchers have to eat."

She shifted on the table. "Spence, I'm sorry, but I can't." She looked at the open door. "How much longer do I have to keep the ice on my foot?"

"Ten more minutes." Ten more minutes to try to convince her to go out with him. It might be the last opportunity he had. "Deena, I really like you, and I think you like me, too. Will you at least tell me the truth about why you won't go out with me?"

She continued to study the floor. "I am telling you the truth," she said at last. "I can't have a relationship with you because of my work."

"Deena, I didn't come here to find a relationship. It was the last thing on my mind, but the more I get to know you, the more I believe God has brought us together for a reason. Don't you?"

Deena considered his question for so long he thought she wouldn't answer. But then she lifted her head and pushed her hair behind her ears. "Spence, I'm here because I chose to come, and so are you. I used to think everything happened for a reason, but then my mom got sick. I believed God could do anything. All you had to do was believe hard enough and ask Him. Well, I asked Him to heal my mother. My whole family, my church, my school, and my town asked Him to spare her, and He didn't. Where was He when my mother was lying in bed in so much pain that you couldn't touch her without making her cry?"

"He was with her, Deena."

"She suffered a lot, Spence."

"He didn't cause the pain."

"But He allowed it. She suffered, Spence, just like thousands of women are suffering every day. I promised my mom I would find a way to help other women with breast cancer."

"I understand you're doing important work, but that doesn't mean you have to sacrifice everything else."

"Sometimes at night I dream about my mother. I wake up at three in the morning. I see her tortured, exhausted eyes. I wasn't in time to help her, but I might be able to help other women."

Spence's heart ached at the sight of Deena's beautiful blue eyes swimming with tears. "I admire what you're doing and your passion for helping others, but, Deena, you don't have to do this alone."

"I have Mr. Crackers."

"He's a nice bird, but he's a bird all the same."

She shifted, and the ice pack fell from her foot. He replaced it and held it there. He had the feeling she'd jump right off the table and run out the door if he didn't hold on to some part of her.

"I'm not as selfless as you think," Deena said flatly. "I told you about my mother, but not about Aunt Betsy or Grandma Dee. They both died of breast cancer, too. Have you ever heard of BRCA1 or BRCA2?"

Spence felt a chill even greater than the one seeping through the ice pack into his hand. "They're genetic tests for breast cancer."

"Yes." Deena swallowed. "Spence, I have BRCA1. My sister and my dad know, but Evie doesn't. Please don't tell her."

Spence released the ice bag, and it fell to the side of her foot. He racked his brain for everything he'd ever read about breast cancer and for something encouraging to say. "That means you have a higher risk of getting cancer than other women, but it doesn't mean you will absolutely get it."

"It means I have a 70 percent chance of developing breast cancer sometime in my life."

"What about surgery? Or drugs like tamoxifen? Isn't that supposed to be a preventive medication?"

She shook her head. "Prophylactic surgery won't guarantee I won't get cancer. And tamoxifen hasn't been proven to help women with BRCA1. BRCA2, yes." She shrugged. "Do you still want to take me to dinner?"

Spence ignored the warning flash in his brain that told him he should think about his answer, take his time and pray about it. "Yeah, I do."

"Well, you shouldn't. What if we got involved, and I got sick? Do you really think you and Alyssa could handle another loss?"

He swallowed. She had a point—one he couldn't simply dismiss. Yet what kind of man would he be to walk away from someone purely because someday she might get sick? "Every relationship is about taking risks, Deena. You don't know what's going to happen. But that's what faith is all about—trusting that God is the One in control and that He has a plan for all of us. A good plan. He doesn't want us to live in fear. Deena, one of the reasons the Lord came was so we could have life—life to its fullest."

"I can live with BRCA1, Spence, but I couldn't bear it if I had a family and they had to watch me go through breast cancer. Trust me, I know what I'm talking about."

Spence sat up straighter. He thought of Evan. "No matter how you lose someone, it hurts. That's just the way it works."

Deena swung her legs over the edge of the table. "I am thirty-five years old. The same age as my mom when she got sick. My sock, please."

He didn't want to give it to her, but she snatched it from his hands. "You can't look me in the eye and tell me you don't have any feelings for me, can you, Deena?"

"It isn't about feelings." Deena stuffed her foot into her sneaker. "It's about doing the right thing. People are counting on me, Spence. You'd just be a distraction."

He jerked as if she'd hit him. A distraction? That was how she saw him? He set his jaw. "I happen to be pretty good at helping people."

"I don't need your help." She limped to the doorway.

"Deena, you're the most accident-prone woman I've ever met in my life." He smiled to let her know he found this aspect of her appealing. "You've hardly gone a day here without needing to be rescued."

Her face darkened like a thundercloud. "You're a nice guy, Spence. When you think about this more, you'll see that I'm right."

"What if I were the one who told you I have a history of heart disease in my family and every male member died before he was fifty years old? Would you turn your back on me?"

Deena frowned. "That's different. And it's not true, is it?"

"No. I'm just trying to make a point. You wouldn't walk away from me. I know you wouldn't. If I had a heart attack, you'd be the first person to give me CPR. You'd be pounding on my chest with your fists and screaming for me to stay away from the light."

He wanted to make her laugh, but she frowned harder. "Spence, there's a child involved. It isn't funny."

"I know, but I'm not scared off, either."

Deena shook her head. "It wouldn't be right."

He clenched his fists. Of course it would be right. He'd make it right; she just had to trust him and have a little faith that God would keep her healthy. He opened his mouth to tell her so then hesitated.

What if she was right? What if he distracted her from her work and therefore delayed or prevented her from developing a treatment?

He wasn't sure what to say, and before he could decide, it was too late. Deena was gone. Spence stared at the empty doorway. He could run after her, but it wouldn't change anything. It wasn't as if he could take away her chances of getting cancer. Just like he couldn't turn back the clock and rescue Evan. He absolutely hated the feeling of helplessness rapidly settling over him, a fog that enveloped him, formless and unfightable. He hated it with a passion.

Looking around his desk, he picked up the first thing he saw—a round pencil holder. He drew his arm back and threw the container against the wall. Pencils flew like small missiles across the room and scattered across the tile floor.

twenty-one

Deena heard the clatter of something falling, but she kept walking. She swiped at the salty tears stinging her eyes. *Fool, she told herself, silly fool. What good is crying over something you can't change? I thought you learned that lesson a long time ago.*

Her throat ached with the effort of holding back the emotions. Work. She'd think about work. About her laboratory. About Quing, Andres, and her other students. She'd think about the most recent group of inhibitors she was studying and. . .anything but Spence. She turned down the hallway and caught a glimpse of bright copper hair just before the door closed.

Evie.

Deena's heart began to thunder in her chest. The girl must have come back from the stable to check on her. Had Evie been eavesdropping? Of course she had, but just how much had she heard? With a sick feeling, she replayed the conversation. She limped faster, ignoring the pain in her bruised toe.

She pushed open the door and squinted into the bright sunlight for a glimpse of her niece. She saw a couple of kids sitting on the grass and two others throwing a football around, and there, at the trailhead, was her niece, her shoulders hunched, her head bent. "Evie! Wait!"

Her niece turned at the sound of her name, but when she recognized Deena, she took off. Deena ran after her, wishing with all her heart that Evie hadn't overheard her conversation with Spence and wondering what she'd say to her when she caught up with her.

Evie had youth and ten good toes, but Deena had longer legs and strength born of desperation. She caught up with Evie, when her niece, proving that she was related to Deena, stumbled over a root on the trail. Evie didn't fall, but in the time it took to regain her balance, Deena caught up with her. "Evie, please, let me explain."

Panting, she faced the girl who stared back at her, red faced and defiant. Evie's light blue eyes locked on Deena's. For a moment the two of them just looked at each other, panting hard. Deena had grown up with everyone telling her she was the spitting image of her mother. She also remembered the feeling when she'd learned she'd inherited more than her mother's black hair and blue eyes. Evie was tall with the same wide jaw and light blue eyes as Deena. She wondered if Evie was seeing their physical similarities and wondering if she, too, had inherited the cancer gene.

"Genetics are complicated," Deena began, struggling to sound professorial and calm and not winded and afraid. "We're just beginning to understand what causes some genes to mutate and what it all means." She stepped closer to Evie, but the girl backed up an equal distance. "I inherited a mutated gene, but like I told Spence, it doesn't mean I'm going to get cancer."

Evie studied the ground. Deena tried again. "Look at me. I'm as strong as an ox." She studied the girl's bent head. "Your mother doesn't have the mutation, so you probably don't, either. We didn't tell you because we didn't want you to worry."

More dead silence. Deena clenched her fists. What else could she say? The truth was what it was. How much more could she sugarcoat it? Couldn't Evie see Deena hated talking about this?

"There are so many more treatments available now than when your grandmother was diagnosed. And detection is so much earlier now, too. That's a really big key in fighting cancer, Evie, catching it early."

Evie looked up. Her blue eyes seemed to have grown two sizes larger. There was an adult expression in them now. "If you're not worried about getting cancer and there's so many good treatments now if you do get it, how come you wouldn't go out with Mr. Spence?" Her chin came up a notch, just like

Stacy's. "I know you like him."

It was Deena's turn to study the ground and feel the burn on her cheeks. She couldn't deny the truth of Evie's words. She lifted her gaze. "It's complicated."

Evie grunted in disgust. "Complicated? I think it's very simple. You're just like my mother. There's the truth, and then there's what she tells me."

"What are you talking about, Evie?"

The girl didn't answer. She backed away from Deena and shook her head, and as if she couldn't bear whatever thoughts were spinning in her mind, she turned and ran.

≈

As Spence considered breaking something else, he realized two things. First, Deena had left her black fanny pack—the one that held Alyssa's rescue inhaler—on the chair. And second, Alyssa hadn't dropped by the clinic that morning for her allergy medications.

She'd gone horseback riding. He couldn't imagine a place more full of allergens. Mold, dust, grasses, animal dander— just to name a few. And she was there, right now, with no rescue inhaler in case she had an asthma attack.

He poked his head into the office next to his and asked Miriam to cover for him. With the medical fanny pack clutched in his hand, he jogged off to the stables.

Less than ten minutes later, he stood in front of the barn. Panting, he wiped the sweat from his forehead and looked around for Alyssa. The setting looked picturesque, a scene from a New England painting. Only there were no signs of either horses or riders. The paddocks were empty and so was the hitching post. Only a few annoying flies buzzed around his head.

His gaze traveled to the thin line trampled in the grass that disappeared into the woods. Were they still on the ride?

For the first time he hesitated. About a month ago Alyssa had forgotten her lunch, so he'd brought it to school. Not trusting the women in the front office, he'd insisted on delivering it himself during her lunch break. The minute she saw him striding toward her table, sack in hand, she'd turned a shade of scarlet and scooted low in her seat as if she were about to slide right under the table.

He didn't look forward to repeating the experience. Well too bad. Alyssa shouldn't be without her medication.

He opened the Dutch doors to the barn and stepped into the semidarkness. A radio playing Willie Nelson and the sound of voices filled the aisles. Moving deeper inside, he walked past horses standing in cross ties as their riders scurried about putting away tack or rubbing their saddle areas dry.

Other horses wearing nothing but halters and lead ropes stood lined up by the wash stall.

He touched the flank of a bay mare and slipped underneath the cross tie. Where was Alyssa? Despite himself, he was starting to get worried. Maybe something had already happened. Then he heard voices coming from inside one of the stalls.

"You're a really good rider, Alyssa," a girl said. "That was so cool when you jumped Jericho over that fallen log."

Alyssa had jumped her horse over a log? He didn't know she could do that. He wasn't sure he would allow her to do it again. Evan used to jump his bike over things, too. Once, he tried to jump it over a garbage can and ended up breaking his collarbone. Spence had needed to run for help.

He started to pull the stall door open but hesitated as he heard Alyssa say, "I used to take lessons. There was this pony, Peanuts, and I was going to lease him. But that was before."

Spence's heart began to hammer. *Before* meant before the car accident. He felt that strange sensation of the strength being drained from his body.

"Did you ask your uncle? He might still let you do it."

"My granny in Texas says if I come live with her I can have my own horse. To own. Not even lease."

"Seriously?"

"Seriously. She lives on this big piece of property with this cool pond you can swim in. And she knows how to drive a four-wheeler."

Spence's heart sank into his shoes. Was bribing Alyssa the only way to keep her? He hated to think of competing with Dixie Everett for Alyssa. There was Evan's life insurance money—he could use that to buy Alyssa a horse, but he didn't want to resort to that.

Maybe he should let her go.

Spence pushed the stall door open. Alyssa and Lourdes sat shoulder to shoulder in a pile of hay. The black-and-white pony lifted its neck and seemed mildly surprised but not displeased to see him. He wished Alyssa's expression were as friendly.

Spence's feet sank into the clean, sweet-scented pine shavings. " 'Lyssa, you forgot to take your allergy medicine this morning. You get a special delivery."

"I don't need it."

"Is Miss Deena okay?" Lourdes asked.

The pony stepped toward him, sniffing his hand for treats. Its breath was warm, the hair soft on its muzzle. "Miss Deena is fine. Her toe is bruised, not broken." He looked at Alyssa, who concentrated fiercely on braiding together three strands of hay. "Come on, 'Lyssa, it'll just take a second."

Without argument, she dropped the braided hay onto the ground. Spence struggled to hide his frustration. She had the look of someone who had just agreed to undergo a root canal. He'd rather have her defy him than give him this blank, almost zombielike acquiescence.

"You want something to wash it down with?" He led her into the office area of the barn and to an ancient-looking soda machine.

"Water's fine."

He fished in his pockets for some change and fed the slot. "So you had fun riding this morning?"

"Yes."

A bottle of water tumbled to the bottom. He twisted the

cap off and handed the bottle to her.

"I didn't know you could ride."

"Well, I can."

"Well, so can I. Maybe we could do it together sometime."

"Our cabin already had its turn." Alyssa took the small white pill and washed it down with a drink. She used the nasal spray but refused the inhaler.

"I mean at home. There's a stable nearby, right?" When she nodded, he added, "So we could go there sometime."

She shrugged. "Sure." She handed him the water.

The way she said it, it wasn't going to happen. Spence wanted to bend down, look her in the eye, and tell her he was hurting, too. That he missed Evan and Mattie all the time. That he wished he could turn back the clock and do things differently. He even would gladly take Evan's place in that car. He feared, though, that sharing his pain would only fuel her own unhappiness. So he pushed back his feelings. Reaching over, he mussed her hair. "Now go have some fun."

It took her half a second to tear out of there, leaving him with the fanny pack of allergy medicine and the knowledge that if God wanted Alyssa to stay with him, He was going to have to step in. Because Spence had no clue what he was doing wrong or how to make things right.

twenty-two

Deena wiggled her big toe, although the movement made it hurt even worse. Part of her welcomed the pain, even foolishly hoped it would wipe out her inner misery. Evie probably hated her. And Spence. She couldn't bear to think how she'd left him. The look of frustration and pain on his face haunted her.

She checked her watch for the millionth time and sighed as Pastor Rich marched back and forth across the amphitheater stage. Only one o'clock, and the rest of the day seemed like forever. She tried to cheer herself up by reminding herself that tomorrow afternoon she and Mr. Crackers would be on their way home.

She tried not to think of what Stacy would say when she brought Evie home. Evie, who now knew all about the gene for breast cancer that ran in their family.

Pastor Rich paced the stage enthusiastically describing the afternoon's event—a camp-wide scavenger hunt—with words such as "awesome" and "amazing." All he needed was to insert "like" every other word and he'd be speaking teen perfectly.

Deena's gaze shifted to the ripples on the lake. Even more than the slight chill on her arms and the grayness of the sky above, the movement of the water announced the coming change in the weather.

A cold front combined with rain was due by evening. She couldn't watch the ripples without thinking the ground beneath her life was just as unsteady, pushed by a wind she couldn't see, leaving her shaken, feeling off balance.

She glanced down the row. Evie, her hair loose and thick as if to look as different from Deena as possible, sat at the very end of their group. Alyssa sat next to her, almost shoulder to shoulder, in a way that spoke as loudly as words that the two of them were friends.

Deena remembered sitting with Stacy like that. She an
her sister had been so close they could practically read eacl
other's minds. It wasn't like that now. They loved each othe
but each led a very different life. She feared the distanc
between them would grow even wider when Deena returne
with Evie tomorrow afternoon.

"Safety comes first," Pastor Rich said loudly. "Everyon
stays together. If I see a camper by himself or herself, he o
she becomes my buddy for the rest of the day." He grinned
"As entertaining as I am, I don't think you want to hang ou
with a middle-aged guy."

She spotted Spence seated a few rows ahead of her. He
gaze rested on the close-cropped hair on the back of his head
For the first time, she thought she understood how frustrating
it had to be for him to watch Alyssa shut down every time he
came near.

"Secondly," Pastor Rich continued, "each item on the
scavenger list has been given a point value. The winning team
will be the one that earns the most points."

Like her team was likely to win. Deena nearly snorted
She'd never seen a group so disorganized in her life. Every
morning somebody was missing something—a hairbrush, a
tube of mascara, a ponytail holder. Taylor and Britty had even
mixed up their matching toothbrushes.

"Thirdly, all items must be brought back to the commissary
to be counted and recorded by 5:00 p.m. No items will be
accepted after the 5:00 p.m. deadline. Okay, cabins, please
send your representative to pick up the clues."

Deena glanced at Evie's profile, willing the girl to meet
her gaze. She wanted to choose Evie, to give Evie something
to acknowledge that she was special to her, but the girl
pretended not to see her. So Deena asked Britty, who was
seated next to her.

The girl nodded and along with about fifteen other kids
hurried down the log steps to the front of the stage.

When all the representatives from the cabins had their envelopes, Pastor Rich asked for the Lord's blessing on the hunt and that He would hold off the rain. Then he raised his hand theatrically in the air. "On your mark," he said. "Get set. . . . Go!" Waving his arm as if it were a checkered flag, he started the hunt.

The kids thundered back to their seats. Despite her misgivings about the activity, Deena found herself leaning forward, shouting encouragement to Britty, who was racing a much bigger boy up the steps.

"Hurry, Brit!" Taylor shouted. Even Evie seemed to come to life, rising to her feet and cheering as Britty passed a girl who had tripped over her shoelaces.

Maybe this scavenger hunt would not be a pointless exercise in futility. Deena closed her eyes. *If You're up there, God, if You can hear me, please let this race bring Evie and me together. Please help us end this camp experience on a good note.*

Breathless, Britty joined them in the seats. She handed Deena the long white envelope. Ripping it open, Deena read aloud:

> *Dear Campers,*
>   *"Seek and you will find" (Luke 11:9).*
>   *We have spent the week learning more about the Lord and about the Bible. Below is a list of Bible-related objects. Good luck on your journey, and may you find that the answers you seek can sometimes be found in the most unusual places.*
>   *God bless each of you,*
>   *Pastor Rich*

> *Scavenger List*
> * *A handmade cross—created without use of tape, string, or nails (10 points)*
> * *A crown of thorns (10 points)*
> * *Something rare and precious (25 points)*
> * *A slice of bread (5 points)*

- *A fish (dead 5 points, alive 10 points)*
- *A seed of faith (5 points)*
- *A Christmas tree (3 points, decorated 10 points)*
- *Four nails (2 points each)*
- *A symbol of hope (5 points)*
- *Something eternal (10 points)*
- *A prayer written by a stranger (15 points)*
- *Living water (10 points)*
- *Body of Christ (5 points)*
- *Blood of Christ (5 points)*
- *Not a her, but a homonym for him + al (5 points)*
- *A bit of truth (5 points)*
- *Life's guidebook (5 points)*
- *Eve's temptation (5 points)*
- *A pillar of salt (5 points)*
- *A praying mantis (15 points)*
- *Ashes (5 points)*
- *An eagle's feather (25 points)*
- *Armor of God (10 points)*
- *Pastor Rich's sunglasses (lost near the amphitheater two days ago, 25 points)*
- *This list, intact, no stains (1 point)*
- *A doughnut (10 points, chocolate 15 points)*

Deena looked up. The girls had pressed around her so tightly that she almost bumped her forehead on Lourdes's chin.

"This is like seriously impossible." Britty's eyes, framed in heavy black eyeliner, blinked furiously. "I mean, how are we going to hold a cross together?"

"Easy." Taylor pulled her wad of bubble gum out of her mouth. "We find two sticks and glue them together with my Dubble Bubble."

A cheer went up from the group. "Next?" Lourdes prompted excitedly. "What's next?"

"If we go in order," Britty said, "it's find a crown of thorns. Where are we going to find that?"

"Ha," Taylor said. "We don't find it—we make it. My gum and your headband. Britt, let's find a rosebush, and we're all set."

"Bubble gum on my headband?" Britty shook her head. "No way."

"We can use one of mine," Alyssa offered, removing a white plastic band from her head.

"And I know where to find a rosebush," Evie shouted. "The baptismal pool!"

"Shh," Lourdes said, holding her finger to her lips. "You want the other teams to hear? Hey, if we get some water from the baptismal pool, that would take care of another clue, too." She grinned, showing a multitude of silver bands. "The living water one."

"You're, like, a genius, Lourdes," Britty said. "Keep going. What's next?"

Around them, kids spoke in excited, overlapping voices, and small groups split off from the bench seats, running in every direction.

"Come on, Miss Deena," Lourdes said, rising to her feet. "We've got a lot of ground to cover."

Two hours later excellent progress had been made. Their team had created a very respectable cross out of twigs and bubble gum. They'd fashioned the crown out of Alyssa's headband and thorns from the rosebushes.

To decorate a Christmas tree, they'd found an evergreen branch and decorated it with Britty's earrings and a chain of Taylor's bubble gum wrappers.

A trip to the commissary had netted several items from the scavenger hunt list: a saltshaker for a pillar of salt, crackers (body of Christ), a can of grape juice (blood of Christ), an apple (Eve's temptation), a can of tuna (fish), a slice of bread, and a package of pumpkin seeds (for a seed of faith).

At the stable they'd retrieved a horse's bit for "a bit of truth" and found four horseshoe nails. They'd figured out that "life's instruction book" was the Bible (which they retrieved from

Lourdes's suitcase) and "not a her, but a homonym for him + al" was a hymnal.

Deciding that the "armor of God" was a life jacket, they raced to the boathouse.

The air had grown even heavier with the coming rain. Deena's lungs labored, and her big toe burned as if it were on fire. She could hardly keep up with the kids, who bounded like deer down the trail. Even Evie seemed to have gotten into the spirit of the competition. Watching her bright copper head lead the way gave Deena a small hopeful feeling. This was like the old Evie, charging ahead, full of enthusiasm.

She gratefully slowed to a walk as they reached the beach area. The girls ran ahead, and she followed slowly, favoring her hurt toe. The huge lake spread in front of her, nearly spanning the parameters of her vision. A line of orange buoys bobbed amid the choppy waves, and the water matched the same dark color as the sky. Leaning her hands on her knees, she managed an out-of-breath greeting as a teenaged boy with a sunburn lifted an empty kayak and hauled it toward the boathouse. He'd almost reached the open door, when a group of boys rushed past him, nearly knocking the kayak from his arms.

"Hey, dudes, careful there."

"Sorry," one of the boys said. Deena recognized him from their tug-of-war match, although she couldn't quite remember his name. The boy didn't sound overly sorry, though, and a moment later he whooped and bumped chests with another boy. The two boys danced in place like football players who had scored the winning touchdown.

A tall boy with long blond hair raised his arm into the air. He had something clutched in his fist. Deena felt her heart sink. She walked over to her group of girls. "Do you see what I see?"

"Yeah." Evie dug the toe of her sneaker into the sand. "Pastor Rich's sunglasses."

"Twenty-five points," Alyssa pointed out. The unofficial accountant, she'd been tallying the score as they went along.

The glasses were worth a lot of points in the scavenger hunt, and no one had to tell the team what this meant. Deena pushed her hair behind her ears. "We can still win, girls. We've found a lot of things on the list."

Britty, who was holding their bag of items, shook her head. "Everything we've found has probably been found by, like, everyone else, too. We really needed to find those sunglasses."

Deena watched the boys continue to dance around the beach. "Give me the list. Let's see if there's another big-ticket item."

She studied the list. "Okay. We've still got a praying mantis, a live fish, a prayer written by a stranger, a chocolate doughnut, something rare and precious, and an eagle's feather." She looked up. "Any ideas?"

"Yeah," Britty said. "We just give up and go back to the cabin and take a nap."

"And eat candy," Taylor added. "Or ice cream. Like we did when we lost the tug-of-war challenge."

"No way are we giving up," Lourdes said. "We can catch a fish, for starters. The prayer of a stranger—I've been thinking, maybe we could use one of David's psalms in the Bible. I mean, no one has actually met David, have they?"

"Well, we know who he is, so he isn't exactly a stranger, is he?" Taylor snapped her bubble.

The girls fell silent. Then Evie said, "We should go after the eagle's feather."

"Where are we going to find an eagle's feather?" Taylor asked.

"Near the eagle's nest," Evie replied. "Across the lake. There's supposed to be a nesting pair near the watchtower. Pastor Rich told us about it, remember?"

Deena looked across the water. Barely visible, but rising from the tree line, she could just make out the brown tower. She frowned. It wasn't a good idea, not with bad weather coming.

"How would we get there?" Lourdes asked.

Evie pointed to the kayaks lying on the sandy beach. "We'll take one of those."

"I'll go with you," Alyssa said.

"It's settled, then," Evie said. "Alyssa and I go after the eagle's feather, and the rest of you should continue looking for the rest of the items on the list."

"I'm sorry, Evie, but no one is going on that lake," Deena said. "The water is a lot rougher than the last time we were out, and it might rain."

Evie lifted her gaze. Her eyes were filled with a yearning and a need that seemed to reach all the way to her soul. "Remember my dream, Aunt Deena? About the eagle? I think we're meant to go."

Deena looked at the rows of waves marching across the water and then up at the gray sky hanging low and heavy with the promise of rain. "No way," she said firmly. "Besides," she added, wanting to soften the look of disappointment on her niece's face, "we can't just take one of these kayaks without asking."

"Then let's ask." Evie's voice had a stubborn note that was pure Stacy. "I saw a staff counselor a moment ago."

As if on cue, the sunburned teenager returned from the boathouse and walked right past them.

"Excuse me," Deena said, hoping to put an end to this conversation. "We can't take out one of the kayaks, can we? The weather and all. . ."

"Have you had safety training?" the boy asked.

"Yes," Evie said eagerly. "And we'll only be gone for a short while."

The boy looked at Deena. "As long as a counselor is in the boat and everyone has had safety training, its okay." He glanced at a fat silver watch on his wrist. "You'd have to be back in an hour, though. That's when I take my break."

"We'd be back in, like, half that time," Evie said confidently.

"But the weather," Deena hinted broadly. "Isn't it a bad idea to take a kayak out when it might rain?" She ignored the death look Evie shot her.

"Oh, it isn't supposed to rain until tonight."

Deena glanced up at the sky. It really didn't look that bad. She probably was being overprotective. After all, from the looks of things, kayaks had been going out all morning. Would taking one out for another hour make much difference? Besides, she didn't want to disappoint the girls, particularly Evie. Deep in her heart Deena believed if she and Evie could just spend more time together, they could get past what had happened this morning.

There would be a headwind, but she was strong. She liked the idea of Evie seeing her physical strength. It would wipe out any notion that Deena might implode at any moment, like a building being demolished. Only in her case, it would be the work of an abnormally dividing cell instead of dynamite.

"Okay," Deena decided. "We'll do it!"

❧

"There's a three-person kayak, Aunt Deena," Evie offered. "Three people can cross that lake more quickly than two."

"I'll go," Alyssa offered. "Evie and I were partners last time." She exchanged nods with Evie. "We make a good team."

Evie was right; they could go faster with three people. If they were really going to do this, it would be better not to waste time arguing. Besides, none of the other girls seemed to want to come. "Could you bring us the three-person kayak?" she asked the teenager.

The sunburned boy grinned and pointed to an orange kayak on the beach. "Make sure you wear your life jackets," he said.

"Okay, then," Deena said after the boy left. "Evie, Alyssa, and I will go after the eagle feather. The rest of you stay here and try to catch a fish. There are fishing poles and nets in the boathouse. And for goodness' sake, don't fall in the water."

"We won't," Britty promised. "But I'm not putting a worm on the hook."

Taylor grinned. "You won't have to. I've got Gummi Worms!"

twenty-three

Deena and the two girls paddled into a fairly steady headwind. There was more of a chop in the water than the last time Deena had been on the lake, but still nothing to worry about. She kept her eyes on the green hills ahead and focused on timing her paddle strokes with Evie's and Alyssa's.

In just minutes her arms began to ache. The wind and current kept trying to push them back to the shore. She had to brace herself with her legs and pull and push with each stroke. In front the girls paddled with determination, ignoring the dull *thunk* of ripples, solid as logs, hitting rhythmically against the bow.

The kayak picked up enough water to soak the bottom of her jeans. She kept paddling, trying not to think about how far away the other side of the lake looked or wonder how deep the water went beneath them.

Deena's grip tightened on her paddle as a gust of wind pushed against the kayak. Something in her welcomed the opportunity to fight against something tangible like the wind. For so many years, she had fought against cancer, a silent enemy that was as stealthy as it was deadly. This wind, though, could be fought against with a stroke of her paddle, and the battle would be won when she reached the shoreline.

They reached halfway, then three-quarters—then the shoreline neared. Deena slowed her paddling as she looked for a safe spot to land the kayak. The tops of slick, black rocks stood between the kayak and a rocky beach. There might be underwater rocks as well. To avoid the rocks, she'd have to land the kayak in a different part of the shoreline. From what she could see, this meant trying to muscle it through the arms of trees growing out from the banks of the water's edge.

Evie looked back, her face flushed and her hair plastered back from wind. "Where?" she yelled.

"To the left. Over there."

"But the trees. . ."

"We'll go between them."

Deena picked a spot between two trees and turned the boat. The wind pushed her too far, though, and Deena found herself pointed between the branches of a leafy tree overhanging the water. Too late to adjust, she yelled for the girls to duck and hoped they could go beneath it.

The idea might have worked, but Deena felt the kayak scrape bottom. A moment later it came to a complete standstill. Caught in the leafy arms of a tree, the kayak rocked in the small waves.

Deena pushed aside a leafy branch. She peered around another. "You okay, girls?"

More branches were pushed aside, and then two heads popped up. "Yeah, we're fine," Evie replied. "Now what?"

"Well, tie the kayak to the tree and let's get going," Deena said. "The watchtower is just above us. We can take a quick look, but we've got to be out of here in ten minutes."

They hopped out of the kayak, gasping and laughing as the knee-high water lapped their legs. Evie sloshed to the front of the kayak and tied its rope around a branch. "To the eagle's nest!"

They dropped their life vests on higher ground. From where they stood, the land rose at a steep pitch from the shore. The pines grew thick and wild, littering the ground with needles, their roots sticking up like knobby knees.

Using small trees and branches for balance, she and the girls started up the hill. The going was slippery. Deena led the way, keeping a sharp lookout for snakes. Several times she had to grab a branch for balance as the needles gave way beneath her feet.

Behind her she heard the labored sound of Evie, or maybe Alyssa, huffing and puffing after her. The cracking of deadwood beneath their feet resonated in the forest. It gave Deena a very bad feeling, as if they were the only living creatures moving about in the woods. It was like everything else knew something they didn't and had taken shelter.

She climbed another fifty yards and reached the lip of the hill, panting hard. There it was. The watchtower, a three-story brown structure, rose high, overlooking the lake and valley behind them.

Moving closer, Deena studied the blistered brown paint on the side rails that looked as though they'd break if even a squirrel leaned against them. The steps sagged, and a lone strand of pine peeked through a tiny gap. No way was she letting either of the girls up that structure.

"Where's the nest?" Alyssa asked, tilting her head to look up at the watchtower.

"It's supposed to be at the top," Evie said. "We just can't see it from the ground."

"Well, you're not going up in the tower," Deena announced. "It's not safe."

"I'm the lightest," Alyssa said. "I could go up there."

"Absolutely not." Deena put her hands on her hips and drew herself up to her full five feet ten inches. When she saw the tilt of Alyssa's chin, she added, "I weigh a hundred forty-five pounds, Alyssa. You do not want me to sit on you, but I will if that's what it takes."

"Well, you're not going then, either," Alyssa said, mirroring Deena's stance right down to the hands on the hips. "I'm only seventy-five pounds, but I can bite like a shark."

Deena hadn't planned to go up herself and blinked in surprise. Just who was protecting whom? She held up her hands in mock surrender. "Okay. None of us are going up there. Let's just look around and see if maybe a feather or two blew out of the nest."

Just in case one of the girls tried to slip into the tower, Deena planted herself at the base of the steps, alternating between checking her watch and staring up at the sky, which seemed to be darkening by the minute. "Hurry up, girls."

The wind had picked up, too. It came in gusts that tore at her hair and plastered her T-shirt to her body. The little swells in the lake below seemed to be moving more quickly as well. She still thought they could make it back before the storm hit.

"Come on," she yelled. "We have to go. Now!"

Evie yelled, "We haven't found it yet. Just give us a few more minutes."

"There is no more time," Deena said, feeling the wind pushing her words back at her. She waited for it to pass, and her gaze fell on something racing across the grass. It was dark, sort of brownish gray. For a moment she thought it might be a rodent, but when it caught beneath a bush, she recognized it for what it was.

"Girls! Come here!"

Evie and Alyssa charged around the side of the tower just as Deena picked up the slim feather. "The wind blew, and suddenly there it was!"

Evie started jumping up and down. "I knew we'd find it!" Taking the object from Deena, she waved it in the air. "Twenty-five points! We're gonna win, win, win!" The two girls grabbed hands and bounced in place.

"You two are going to make it rain," Deena teased. "Come on, guys, let's get out of here."

Slipping and sliding and leaving long trails of black earth exposed where their heels dug into the ground for balance, they raced back to the shoreline. Descending the hill took far less time than climbing it had, and soon they found themselves at the base of the tree growing out over the water.

"Where's the kayak?" Alyssa looked at Deena, who suddenly had a very sick feeling in her stomach. "Is this the right spot?"

"Yeah." Nature girl she wasn't, but Deena was positive this was where they'd left the kayak. Her gaze moved to Evie. She didn't like her train of thought, but Evie had been the one to tie up the kayak. Had she deliberately not tied it tightly enough?

"Look!" Alyssa cried, pointing.

Across the water, the empty kayak rocked in the waves. It had turned sideways and was moving steadily away from them. Silhouetted against the gray water, it had a lost, abandoned look to it, like a ghost ship about to disappear into the mist.

"This is all my fault," Evie cried. "I didn't tie it tight enough. I'm so sorry, Aunt Deena. It was an accident. I swear it was an accident."

Deena remained silent. She couldn't help but think of all the pranks Evie had played, and she knew the girl was still angry with her.

Evie tugged at her hair. "You have to believe me!"

Deena studied her niece's face. The fear and dismay in her eyes seemed real. If the child was faking, she deserved an Academy Award. She sighed. "I believe you, Evie. I know it was an accident."

"Now everyone is going to hate me!" Evie put her face in her hands. "We're losing the scavenger hunt because of me!"

"Evie, that isn't true. No one is going to blame or hate you." Deena stepped closer to her niece. She wanted to hug Evie, yet she held back. She hated this inner reserve in herself, but it was ingrained and impossible to dismiss. She patted the girl's shoulder. "Don't worry."

"No wonder Mom wanted to send me away," Evie said bitterly. "I'm a horrible person. I don't blame her a bit."

Deena's hand froze on her niece's shoulder. What was Evie saying? Stacy adored this child. "Your mother didn't send you away because she doesn't love you. My goodness, Evie, just the opposite. She was more than willing to put her health and the baby's health at risk to come with you to camp."

Evie looked at her, near tears. "I heard you and Mom talking about me, how Mom couldn't have me home anymore because I was too much for her." Her lip trembled, and her gaze dropped. "She wants another boy. I heard her say that to my dad. It's true!"

Alyssa stepped closer and put her hand on Evie's other

shoulder in a show of silent but heartfelt support. Deena studied the top of her niece's head. Stacy did hope for another boy, but not for the reasons Evie believed. It was the genetics Stacy feared. How did she tell Evie the truth without scaring her, though?

"Your mother loves you more than she loves her own life," Deena said. "And that's the truth you need to hold on to."

"How can I trust you?" Evie stepped away from Deena. A branch popped beneath her foot, and the sound of it breaking was cruel and final. "You lied to me about yourself. You didn't tell me about the cancer stuff."

"I never lied," Deena corrected. "We were just waiting for you to get older. You're so young, Evie. We didn't want you to worry, to have to carry this burden. When we get home, you, your mom, and I will talk everything over. I promise."

Even with the breeze now steadily rolling off the water, Deena felt herself sweat. The expression on her niece's face nearly broke her heart. All the boldness, the cockiness that was Evie had drained right out of her. She looked so young, so unsure, so afraid.

Deena remembered staring up at her father like that, wanting comfort and watching him back away from her. She didn't want to be like him, to hold people at arm's distance.

She opened her arms and pulled Evie next to her. When this didn't seem enough, she reached out with her right arm and drew Alyssa into their embrace.

"It's going to be okay," Deena said.

"Yeah," Alyssa agreed. "We're having an adventure. This is much more fun."

Evie wiped her eyes and squirmed out of the group hug. She squared her shoulders. "I'm going to swim out to the kayak and tow it back."

"Over my dead body." Deena lifted her chin. "We're hiking back to camp."

"Uncle Spence says if you're lost in the woods, you should stay right where you are and someone will come find you."

Deena smiled reassuringly. "We aren't lost, Alyssa. All we have to do is follow the shoreline, and it'll bring us right to camp. Hopefully we'll be back before anyone starts to worry about us."

twenty-four

A trail led from the watchtower to the campground. Deena remembered seeing the thin white line on a map. They'd hiked partially there on the first day they had come to the camp—the day they'd wandered into the patch of poison ivy.

The best plan seemed to be to find that trail. As they began the hard work of climbing the hill, she heard drops of rain splattering on the leaves. A fat bead plopped onto her nose.

She climbed faster.

The drops fell more frequently, and then there was a rush as if someone had turned the handle of a faucet to full volume.

Deena looked around for shelter. Blinking as a steady stream of rain pounded over her head, she spotted an overhanging rock half buried in the hill and herded them beneath it. It wasn't much, but it was better than nothing.

Deena pressed both girls into the small crevice and shielded them with her body. The rain battered the earth, bringing with it a darkness that virtually eliminated the last bits of daylight. She shut her eyes, held the girls, and felt the rain pound her back. Deena wished with all her heart that she'd never allowed the girls to talk her into searching for the eagle's feather. She wished she'd never volunteered to take Stacy's place. Ever since she'd arrived, things had gone wrong. She'd come to this camp thinking herself a fairly strong person. Now, huddled beneath this rock, she felt small and helpless. She pressed deeper into the crevice and hugged the girls more tightly. If anything happened to Alyssa or Evie, she'd never forgive herself.

She couldn't tell how much time had passed before the rain eased and the woods quieted. The sky cleared, and a glimmer of sunshine appeared behind a layer of clouds. Deena straightened and pushed her wet hair back. Her shorts wer[e] soaked, and she could have wrung out her shirt. The worl[d] also had changed. The trunks of trees were stained almost black, and the leaves gleamed a glossy green color.

"Wow. That was so cool!" Evie emerged next, also soaked, but grinning. "Kind of scary, too. Were you scared, 'Lyssa?"

Alyssa's honey-colored hair lay plastered to her skull. Her face had a white, pinched look that Deena didn't like. Worst of all, when she opened her mouth, no sound came out. She flapped her arms and looked at Deena with clear panic in her eyes.

The girl was having an asthma attack.

Deena reached for her fanny pack and realized she wasn't wearing it. In a flash of horror, she remembered taking it off in Spence's clinic earlier that morning. In her mind's eye, she saw it sitting on the black vinyl chair.

Alyssa's rescue inhaler was in that fanny pack. Now here she was, in the middle of nowhere, with no inhaler and a girl in trouble. A fear like none Deena had ever felt in her life shot through her veins.

Please, God. Help her breathe.

Deena bent low and grabbed Alyssa's small hands. "Honey, you've got to listen to me." Her voice sounded steady, but on the inside it was screaming, *Oh God, oh God, oh God*, like a distress signal from a sinking ship.

Alyssa made a long, whistling noise. Her eyes had the sick look of an animal caught in a trap. Deena gripped the girl's hands more tightly. *Please, God. I can't do this alone.* "Try to calm down. Slow and easy breaths."

"What should I do?" Evie shouted. "What should I do?"

"Pray." Deena struggled to keep her voice calm. "Alyssa, you're going to be fine. Close your eyes and listen to my voice."

"Heavenly Father," Evie began, "You are a great God. You can do anything. Please help Alyssa breathe. Help her, God. She needs You. Please, God, help Aunt Deena save Alyssa.

Please, God, please. I'm so sorry for all the things I've done wrong. We need You so much. . . ."

Deena continued gripping Alyssa's hands. She'd never been responsible for someone else's life. Nothing in her training had prepared her for the terror or the helplessness she felt as she watched Alyssa struggling for breath. She was all alone. There was no one to turn to. No one to help her. And then something inside her told her she was wrong.

A feeling of quiet peace settled over her, and energy seemed to flow into Deena's ice-cold hands. She heard herself say, "Breathe in through your nose, Alyssa, and out through your mouth. Slowly. Like I'm doing."

Alyssa's chest heaved with the effort. She produced a thin, wheezing noise.

"That's it. Another one."

Alyssa managed another breath.

"You're doing good, honey." A bead of water from Deena's hair plopped onto Alyssa's face. She wiped it off. "Breathe in. . . one, two, three. Now breathe out. . .one, two, three."

Some of the panic receded from Alyssa's face as she followed Deena's order. "Breathe in. One, two, three, four. . ."

Evie finished praying and began reciting Bible verses. Deena continued to coach Alyssa's breathing, taking heart as the color slowly returned to the girl's lips. When she was finally satisfied that Alyssa was truly past the attack and breathing normally, she sat back.

She looked at Alyssa for a long time and then at Evie. She studied the shadows deepening in the woods. She thought about how she had turned away from God after her mother died. How she'd believed once the door was closed between herself and God, it could not be fully opened again. And yet that wasn't true at all. He had been close, just waiting for her to call out to Him. She might have given up on Him, but He hadn't given up on her—not at all.

She reached for Alyssa's hand and then one of Evie's. She bowed her head, and the three of them prayed.

twenty-five

A glance at her watch told Deena they had about four hours to make it back to camp before total darkness. It would be plenty of time, she told herself, as long as the path they were following was the right one. The storm seemed to have passed, but the sky was overcast, the forest draped in shadow. There was enough light to follow the twisting path through the woods, but at the same time Deena felt the darkness coming.

Behind her, the girls trudged along single file. They walked in silence broken only by the sound of their feet crunching over the underbrush and the occasional slap as a mosquito landed on them.

Furtive scurrying noises came from the underbrush, and louder cracking sounds suggested larger, heavier animals roaming. Deer probably, Deena told herself, but she couldn't help imagining a huge black bear silently tracking them, or maybe a hungry bobcat.

If an animal jumped out at them, how would she defend the girls? She thought longingly of Spence, who would know what to do. But that gave no comfort because Spence wouldn't have gotten himself into this position in the first place. She, with all her years of education, with all her awards and degrees and training, had proven to be stupid beyond words.

And yet, a small contrary voice insisted, hadn't something truly amazing happened because they had come? Hadn't she felt some kind of presence, some kind of power flow into her as she'd helped Alyssa? That couldn't have been an adrenaline rush. It couldn't have been.

It was growing darker. How long had it been since their shadows had disappeared? She paused to check on the girls, and a flicker of light in the distance caught her eye. At first she thought it was a big firefly, but then she saw the light was constant, only giving the illusion of turning on and off as it passed through the woods.

Her heart leaped in her chest. "Girls, look." She pointed behind them.

"What?" Evie asked.

"It's a flashlight." She cupped her hands around her mouth. "Over here!" She paused. "Over here!"

A muffled shout drifted back.

Evie and Alyssa added their voices to Deena's.

The light moved closer. They continued to shout back and forth. The voice that replied grew more distinct and definitely familiar.

"Uncle Spence," Alyssa announced, joy evident in her voice.

The light moved faster. They tracked the figure jogging through the woods. The light grew larger as it drew closer, and they glimpsed Spence, a large, dark figure in a rain poncho. He closed the last stretch of trail between them and stood breathing hard, shining the light on each of them. He didn't speak for a moment, but Deena felt the fear and relief rolling almost tangibly off him. Deena blinked back tears. She had never been so grateful to see someone in her entire life.

"Everybody okay?" Spence hardly had the breath to get the words out.

Alyssa flung herself into his arms and hugged him hard. "You came. You found us. Oh, Uncle Spence. . ."

The light dipped and fell to the ground as Spence bent and hugged Alyssa. He enveloped her in his arms, obscuring her completely. He kept his arms around the girl even as he asked Evie and Deena if they were okay. Finally, he released Alyssa and retrieved the light from the ground.

"You sure you two are okay?"

"Yeah," Deena replied.

He swept the light over Deena. She folded her arms, embarrassed by what he must see—her soaked hair and torn clothing and the scratches on her arms.

"Hold on," he said, lifting the poncho out of the way and pulling out his cell phone. "I have to call off the search party."

He spoke a few curt words into the cell phone, assuring whoever was on the other end, probably Pastor Rich, that everybody was okay. Everyone must have been frantic looking for them. She'd probably ruined the scavenger hunt for everyone, not to mention how scared Britty, Taylor, and Lourdes must have been.

Spence clicked the phone shut and replaced it in his pocket. "What happened? Just before the awards ceremony, the camp staff notified us three people had not returned from taking a kayak on the lake, and Britty told me you guys had taken the kayak to the watchtower."

"We went looking for an eagle feather," Alyssa informed him. A small note of pride entered her voice. "We found one, too."

His gaze shot back to Deena, who felt disapproval slicing through the distance between them. "What in the world were you doing looking for an eagle's feather?"

"It was an item on the scavenger hunt list," Deena explained, realizing how lame that sounded. "Look, maybe we should get back to camp before we talk any more about this."

"In a minute." He stepped closer to Deena. "You took the girls out in the kayak when you knew a storm was expected? And then led them on a wild-goose chase in the woods? All for an eagle's feather?" His voice rose on the last part of the sentence.

"It wasn't a wild-goose chase," Alyssa said. "We found the feather. And we would have made it back before the storm, but our kayak came untied."

"It was half sunk by the time I reached it." There was no disguising the anger in Spence's voice. "Do you know what I thought?"

"I'm so sorry we scared you," Deena said.

"I thought you had all drowned," Spence continued, his voice rising. "If I hadn't seen the life jackets on the shore, I'd have been dredging the lake."

"I'm sorry," Deena repeated.

"And not just me," Spence continued, "but just about every cabin counselor is out looking for you all."

"It was an accident," Deena tried again.

"It was sheer irresponsibility." Spence's voice rose, and he punctuated the sentence with a sound of disgust. "That no one got hurt is a miracle."

"It *was* a miracle, Uncle Spence," Alyssa said eagerly. "I had an asthma attack, and we realized my inhaler was left in your office. But Miss Deena helped me, and we all prayed. God helped us."

Spence's gaze swung to Alyssa as if to make sure she was really okay. He gripped the girl's slim shoulders. "You had an attack? And you didn't have an inhaler?" Above the girl's head, he gave Deena a look of disgust.

Deena swallowed the lump in her throat. "I'm sorry. I'm so sorry."

"You never should have gone out on that kayak in the first place. And then not bringing along the inhaler?" He tore at his hair. "How could you have let that happen?"

"Because I left my fanny pack in your clinic, Spence?"

He glared at her. "Are you trying to tell me this is my fault?"

"Of course not. I'm just trying to explain."

"Uncle Spence, it wasn't Miss Deena's fault."

"We'll talk about this later, Alyssa."

Releasing his niece, Spence pushed past Deena and began to lead them down the trail. "Stay close behind," he said to Alyssa in a gentle voice. It changed completely as he addressed Deena. "You go last."

She winced at the coldness in his voice but made no move to defend herself. He was right. She had acted irresponsibly. Alyssa could have died. And it would have been all her fault. She pressed her lips together to keep them from trembling. The glow of her newfound faith began to fade. Her feet hurt, and Spence hated her. What had seemed like an act of God now seemed exactly what Spence had said, an act of irresponsibility.

She never should have come to this camp. She should have stayed in the safety of her lab. She had tumor specimens to study, cells to stain, promising combinations of powerful cancer cell inhibitors to test and study.

She wanted to go back to her old life where work was all that mattered. The trouble was, she didn't think she was that same person anymore.

twenty-six

They arrived back at camp shortly after eight o'clock. The first thing Deena saw was the tall poles of the Leap of Faith apparatus. It was empty of campers now. She heard the music coming from the amphitheater, suggesting the campers were having their evening devotional. She was glad there were no campers to see them. No one to witness her shameful return. She would not have to see her failure reflected in their eyes.

They passed the commissary, and Spence led them to the single-story building that housed the administrative offices. Every light was burning as Spence marched straight to Pastor Rich's office.

Britty, Taylor, and Lourdes were seated on the senior pastor's ancient leather couch. When they saw them, the girls shouted with joy and leaped up to greet them with fierce hugs and cries of how worried they had been.

Pastor Rich hung up the telephone. A broad grin spread over his round face. "Thank God," he said. "Are you all okay?"

"Yes, Pastor Rich." Deena explained what had happened and took full responsibility for the accident. When the girls tried to intercede on her behalf, she just talked louder and faster.

When she finished, Pastor Rich sat back and steepled his fingers. "Well, that was some adventure. You had us all worried. I was just calling your sister, Deena, when you walked in. We've never lost anyone before at Camp Bald Eagle, and I'm glad you all weren't the first."

"I apologize," Deena said. "And of course, you'll want me to step down as cabin counselor."

"Deena, even if camp wasn't ending tomorrow, I still wouldn't want you to quit. It's not the way we do things here." His gaze turned to Spence. "I'm glad you found them, Spence. Your search-and-rescue skills were a real blessing to us today." He looked at Deena. "He had us all organized in search parties and out looking for you within thirty minutes."

Spence nodded. "I'm just glad it all worked out."

"I am, too," Pastor Rich said. "Now you all are probably tired and hungry. My wife is heating a pot of stew for you in the kitchen. The biscuits are a bit tough, though. Just a friendly warning."

They could have been serving prime rib for all Deena cared. Alyssa and Evie probably were starving, though. She turned to leave. "Hold on a second, Deena," Pastor Rich said. "There's one more thing."

She paused.

"We all make mistakes," the pastor said gently. "We forgive others as we want God to forgive us." He looked at her as if he understood that most of all Deena would have a hard time forgiving herself. "Talk to God about this, Deena. You'll see that He loves you no less. And neither do I."

She drew her trembling fingers through her hair, still cold and damp from the rain. Would Spence forgive her as well? Her heart began to pound. She turned slowly, afraid to look but unable to stop herself.

Both Spence and Alyssa were gone.

twenty-seven

As if to make up for the day before, the Connecticut morning was picture perfect. The sky wrapped the earth in a shade of light blue, the temperature was in the seventies, and the air smelled clean and fresh.

The powerboat rocked gently in the small swells of the lake as Spence climbed inside. Stationing himself in the back, he watched the girls wade into the lake.

As its name suggested, the long, yellow inflatable looked exactly like a big banana. A long cable connected it to the powerboat.

The girls gasped at the temperature of the water and climbed aboard the raft as fast as they could.

Alyssa mounted the yellow tube with a boost from Evie, who then settled herself in front of his niece. "Let's make like a banana and split!" Evie yelled.

Spence's grin faded as Deena stepped out of the boathouse and headed straight for them. She wore a sleeveless white shirt, a pair of red shorts, and a red baseball cap.

He felt disgusted with himself, yet he couldn't make himself look away as she walked onto the pier.

The bruise on her cheek had faded, but she had numerous cuts and scratches on her arms. Spence wanted to both heal them and use them to remind himself of Deena's irresponsibility. She had endangered Alyssa. He forgave her as his faith required, but that didn't mean he'd be quick to forget.

"I know you think I don't deserve to be here," Deena said, joining him in the back of the boat. "Believe me, I wouldn't have come if the girls hadn't insisted."

"You won the skit challenge. You deserve this as much as anyone." He pretended to take great interest in the way the girls had arranged themselves on the banana boat and firmly ignored the part of him that wanted to watch Deena strap on the life vest.

"Britty," Deena shouted. "Did you remember to take out your earrings?"

"Yes, Miss Deena."

"Taylor? No bubble gum, right?"

Spence's gaze swung to Taylor. He hadn't thought of stuff like that. "No bubble gum," the girl confirmed.

"Everybody ready?" Pastor Rich called from the wheel of the boat.

"Yes," Spence said. As soon as this was over, he'd go back to the clinic and finish packing.

The engine coughed to life and the floorboards began to rumble. A moment later they began pulling away from the pier, dragging the banana boat along behind.

The girls screamed as cold water rose over their knees. The boat picked up speed as they left the dock. Alyssa's long, honey-colored hair streamed behind her, and her mouth opened in joy. She had her arms wrapped around Evie, who had her head thrown back laughing.

Spence wished Evan could see Alyssa. His heart ached for all the moments of this girl's life his brother would miss. He vowed not to miss a single thing himself if he could help it.

The boat accelerated, sending cool air rushing past his ears. Trees and boulders along the shoreline passed in a blur of greens and the flash of silver rock.

Behind them the big yellow inflatable bounced in the wake. The girls clung to the small handles. The boat leaned into a wide U-turn. It wasn't a steep pitch, but Deena, who had been holding on to her hat, lost her balance and bumped into Spence. Instinctively his arm shot out to steady her. As the boat continued to turn, she pressed against his side, leaning the full length of herself against him. For a few seconds they were agonizingly close, and Spence thought he'd have to either kiss her or jump overboard. Then Deena's hat flew off.

"Hat overboard," Spence shouted, not caring a bit about the baseball cap but welcoming the excuse to focus on something besides the feel of Deena against him.

Pastor Rich cut the engine, and the boat came to a slow idle. "Do you see it?"

"Over there." Deena pointed.

Spence caught a glimpse of red among the ripples in the water.

"Want me to swim over and get it?" Evie yelled.

"No," Deena and Spence shouted at the same time. "Pastor Rich will bring the boat around, and I'll fish it out," Spence yelled.

"It's just a hat," Deena protested. "You don't have to get it back."

Spence looked at all the colors in her face. Blue eyes, red lips, white teeth, and tanned skin. She dazzled him, thoroughly and completely. Yet he couldn't pursue a relationship with her. After yesterday he'd understood this. Understood that being a father would mean making personal sacrifices. As the pastor slowly brought the boat into position, Spence pulled out the fishnet.

"I'm sorry."

"No big deal," Spence replied.

"Not just about the cap. I'm sorry about yesterday. I tried to explain last night, but I couldn't find you."

"There's no need," Spence said, his own voice sounding as if someone had shoved a cheerful note into it by force. "I accepted your apology yesterday."

"I want to tell you," Deena said in a low, serious tone, "that what I did, taking the kayak out and all, was wrong. But, Spence, something really amazing happened last night. I don't think any of us will be the same."

Spence already knew this. He'd known it since the night before when he'd stood at the door to Alyssa's cabin and she had looked up at him. Really looked at him in a way she hadn't since that first day he'd shown up. To his amazement, she'd asked him to pray with her before she went inside.

"Look. You don't need to go into this any further," Spence said. They'd neared Deena's cap, bobbing about like a red turtle. He fished it out and handed it to her, dripping wet.

Deena took it gingerly, wrinkling her nose. "It smells like a dead fish."

The girls in the banana boat laughed. Spence's gaze stayed on Alyssa the longest. She looked tiny tucked between Evie and Lourdes.

"You all ready?" Spence yelled.

"Ready," the girls shouted.

The line between the powerboat and inflatable tightened, and the banana boat jerked forward. Spence kept his gaze peeled on the cluster of girls and appreciated the rush of wind and the roar of the motor that prevented him from further discussion with Deena.

Alyssa gave him a thumbs-up sign. He gave her the same, although it took quite a bit not to yell that she should keep holding on to the handle and not be waving at him.

Yet he'd been given very specific instructions that morning. "Uncle Spence," she'd said when she came to his clinic for her morning medications, "if you come with us on our reward trip this morning, please don't ask me if I'm feeling okay, or wearing enough sunscreen, or drinking water regularly. I'm not a little kid."

From his perspective, she was a little kid. "Okay," he'd agreed. "I'll just bring my stethoscope and blood pressure cuff."

"This isn't funny," Alyssa said and gave him a piercing look that reminded him so much of Evan that he couldn't breathe for a moment. "And in the future when I'm around my friends, please don't make a big deal about my health. Don't fuss over me. It's embarrassing. And unnecessary." She'd given him a calculating look. "Miss Deena doesn't do it."

"In the future," Spence had repeated casually as if his mind had not already leaped to its own conclusion about what those three words meant. "As in the rest of the week, or as in. . . something more permanent?"

"More permanent." Her gaze dropped to the floor.

With those two simple words, Spence felt his life change forever. A change that both thrilled him and scared him to death. He was pretty good at rescuing people, but sticking around them afterward, that was new territory.

Pastor Rich began a series of turns. Spence's jaw tightened as the banana boat jumped the wake and caught a good two feet of air. The girls screamed bloody murder as the boat slapped down.

"Are we supposed to be going this fast?" Deena shouted, her hair wild and her eyes bright.

"Yeah," Spence shouted back, although he'd been thinking the same thing.

If any one of those girls fell off that banana, he'd be in the water immediately. In that moment, he realized he would not be going to medical school. God had called him to be a paramedic, and that was what he would continue to do. He'd find work that wouldn't take away from his time with Alyssa, but he'd stay an EMT. When the camp finished, he'd start looking for another paramedic job in Winsted.

He pushed his sunglasses more firmly onto his face. They would begin building the life he and Alyssa had discussed that morning.

"You sure you want to stay with me?" he'd asked.

"Yes."

Spence had bent to look her in the eye. Eyes that were the same color and shape of Evan's. And his, too.

"What about Texas?"

She shrugged. "What about it?"

Spence ignored the voice telling him not to push. "What's changed?"

Silence. He didn't think he could bear it if she put up that wall between them again.

"Me," she said. "That's what's changed. When I had that asthma attack, I realized I didn't want to die."

Spence had felt the hair on the back of his neck stand bolt

upright. A panic like he'd never encountered on any rescue mission shot through him. "Alyssa," he said gently, "you weren't thinking of killing yourself, were you?"

"No," she'd said. "Not physically. But if I went to Texas, I think part of me would have died, too." She looked up at him, her eyes looking far older than her twelve years. "I really wanted to live with you, Uncle Spence, but I felt like I didn't deserve it."

"What?" Spence had heard her clearly, but her words made no sense to him. "Why would you think that?"

Alyssa's gaze dropped to the tile floor. Spence gently placed his finger under her chin and lifted her face.

"Because it was all my fault." Her mouth trembled. "The accident."

"Alyssa," Spence said, "none of that was your fault."

She shook her head. "I should have been with them. In that car. Only I was reading this book I wanted to finish. I argued and argued and finally they let me stay home." She looked up at him. "If I'd been with them, it would have changed the timing. They wouldn't have been in that exact place at that exact time. They'd still be alive."

If, if, if. How many times had Spence said the same thing to himself? If only he had been more direct with Evan, shared his concerns instead of fearing he would hurt his brother's feelings. If only he had insisted that Evan get help for his drinking. If only he'd called for a family intervention.

"One more loop," Pastor Rich shouted, bringing Spence back to reality.

He glanced at Deena, wild haired and flushed from the wind and speed of the ride. He wondered if he'd done the right thing, telling Alyssa that Evan had been drinking and this had been a contributing factor in the accident. He had not told Alyssa that her father had been intoxicated or that he had a drinking problem. His goal had been to free Alyssa from her guilt. She'd cried, and so had he. The first tears since Evan had passed away.

He wanted to tell Deena, but this new bond with Alyssa

seemed much too new and fragile. Plus he felt compelled to protect his brother in death, even as he had not in life.

The boat completed its final loop and slowly glided toward the shore. As the sandy beach neared, Spence turned to Deena. "In case things get crazy and I don't see you before we leave this afternoon, I just want to thank you for all you've done for Alyssa. She's not the same girl as the one who arrived."

"I know." Deena looked into his eyes. "And she's got the poison ivy spots and bug bites to prove it."

"And she's got a good friend in Evie," Spence said. "I think they're going to stay in touch."

The boat came to a gentle stop, and Pastor Rich cut the engine. The sudden quiet seemed loud in Spence's ear. What about them? Did he want to stay in touch with Deena? He read the question in Deena's eyes and let his silence be the answer.

He busied himself with reeling in the banana boat, glad for the feel of the thick cable in his hands. The inflatable drifted closer, and when the water became shallow enough, the girls hopped off.

The next time he looked at Deena, she was halfway out of the boat. Their eyes met, and his heart hammered in his chest. It would take so little to open that door between them.

He glimpsed her straight back and glossy, wind-blown hair. Then she walked down the long arm of the pier and out of his life.

twenty-eight

Only a few hours remained before the buses left camp and took her back to her old life. Deena gathered her beach bag from the boathouse. Most of her packing had been completed early this morning, but she had no desire to go back to the cabin and pretend everything was okay.

Because it wasn't. She wasn't. She wasn't sure who she was anymore or what she wanted in life. Yesterday she'd felt the door reopening on her faith, and with it she had let herself start to believe God had a plan for her—a plan that actually included a family.

She walked more briskly down the needle-laden path. All these years she'd been telling herself relationships were distractions and the responsibilities that came along with them would keep her from giving the best of herself to her work. It had all been lies, though, lies that protected her from being vulnerable to someone, from letting people get too close.

Yet despite these very strong walls she'd built around herself, Spence had gotten close to her.

She passed the archery field with the targets neatly lined up, waiting for the next group of campers. The pool was empty, as were the volleyball courts and the horseshoe pits.

Just what was she supposed to do now? If God had a plan for her life, why was He so mysterious about it? Couldn't He just come right out and tell her what to do?

Deena found herself at the base of the Leap of Faith. She stared up at the telephone pole and thought about the time when Spence had soared through the air like Superman. Evie, too, had successfully completed the jump.

"Hey. Can I help you?"

Deena jumped at the sound of a man's voice. Turning, she

saw a teenager wearing a nylon vest with a coil of rope slung over his shoulder. "Oh no. I was just looking."

"Because if you wanted to, you could try it. I haven't started taking everything apart yet."

"Oh no. No thank you." She started to walk away and then hesitated. This exercise—it was all about learning to deal with fear. Deena touched the hard surface of the wooden pole. Suddenly she was tired—so tired of living with all the fears she kept bottled up inside her.

"You have to put a harness on if you're going to climb," the boy said. He had one in his hands as if he'd known all along she'd try it.

Deena stepped into the nylon straps and held her breath as the young man pulled the straps tight around her. She didn't flinch as he clipped the safety rope to her back. "Okay, you're all set."

The first rung felt warm and reassuringly solid. It felt right to be doing this, as if she was meant to do it.

Halfway up it felt less right. In fact, she felt awfully woozy. Looking up at how high she still had to climb made her stomach shrivel to the size of a raisin. She didn't dare look down. The rungs slipped in her sweaty palms, yet she was afraid to let go and wipe her hands on her shorts.

The higher she went, the more wobbly the pole became. No one had prepared her for this. No one had warned her that the pole would shake as if moved by a small earthquake. It made her angry. She used the anger to keep moving.

Finally, her hands found the top of the pole. She traced the pole's flat surface, no bigger than a dinner plate. The anger disappeared, and in its place the fear returned, roaring in her ears like a jet engine.

Replacing fear with faith was the point of this exercise. She had to find her faith. There was a harness on her back. Even if she lost her balance, the safety line would keep her from falling to the ground.

Gathering her courage, Deena pulled herself onto the top

of the pole. There wasn't much space, but she managed to get both her hands and her feet onto the circle of wood. For an agonizing few seconds she posed with her rear end skyward, the pole swaying slightly and her own fear bringing bile to the back of her throat.

She had to look ridiculous from the ground, perched like this. Yet Deena didn't think she could let go. She'd stay in this yogalike position until one of her muscles cramped or they sent the helicopter to come and get her. *Faith, Deena. Find your faith.*

She stood up.

The world swayed. She glimpsed the ground a million miles away. Moving her eyes increased the feeling of vertigo. She reached her arms out, but there was nothing to help steady her.

The trapeze hung just a few feet away. She should jump for it before she lost her balance completely. Before she lost her nerve. *Dear God,* Deena prayed. *I'm letting go.*

The world dropped away from her. She stretched out her arms like Wonder Woman and with a rush of adrenaline flew through the air. The trapeze bar rushed closer and closer. A second later, her hands smacked painfully onto the hard, round pole. Her fingers frantically scrambled, but she had too much momentum. The pole slid out of her grasp.

In the blink of an eye, Deena felt herself falling. A second later, she felt the jerk of the safety line and found herself hanging like a giant fish suspended just above the safety net.

"You did great," the boy said, managing somehow to sound sincere, excited even, as he lowered her slowly. "You almost made it. Want to try again?"

Deena shook her head. She hadn't done great. She'd failed. All those fears she wanted to replace with faith were still firmly attached to her. Just look at her, trembling like a leaf. It would be a miracle if her legs would even hold her upright.

Earlier she'd asked for answers, and she'd gotten them.

Deena was going home.

twenty-nine

Deena keyed in the code to the cell culture lab and pushed open the door. She'd only been gone eight days, but it seemed much longer. She felt as though she were stepping into the room for the first time, looking around and taking in all the sights.

She pulled her lab coat from its peg on the back of the door and slipped it on, then donned a pair of latex gloves. The room seemed quieter than she'd remembered. It was a good quiet, though, a good thinking kind of quiet. Problem solving. Troubleshooting. Figuring out which tumors would react to what treatments. This was what she had always loved about her work.

She flicked on the UV light to prepare a sterile area behind the glass hood and removed a subculture plate from the incubator. She gathered a few more supplies—her pipettes and the nutrients she would insert into the cancer samples that would keep the cells alive—and sat down to get to work.

The next time she looked up, it was six o'clock. Driving home, she almost stopped at a pizza parlor for a pepperoni pie, but she wouldn't let herself. It would only remind her of eating pizza with Spence. She needed to put him and everything associated with him behind her.

In her condo, Deena popped a frozen dish of macaroni and cheese into the microwave. Maybe not the best nutritional choice, but she really needed comfort food.

As the dish heated, she wondered how Stacy was doing, if the heart-to-heart talk had worked and if her sister's relationship with Evie had improved. The night camp had ended, she and her sister had sat down and talked. Deena had shared Evie's fears of not being loved as much as the new baby. Stacy had been shocked, then hurt, then resolved to make things better between herself and Evie.

Deena turned on the television for background noise. When the microwave pinged, she removed the dish and poured herself a glass of filtered water from the refrigerator. She wondered how Spence and Alyssa were doing, if they were eating dinner right at this very moment.

From the living room, she heard a man's voice on the television inviting watchers to call an 800 number if they had been involved in a car accident and were seeking compensation.

From his perch, Mr. Crackers squawked, "Call 203-555-3393."

Deena threw away the plastic covering the macaroni. "That's not even the right number," she said.

She carried her dinner back into the living room and plopped down on the couch. She stirred the gummy pasta with her fork. The news returned, bringing with it disasters happening around the world. Deena barely listened.

Everything was exactly as she'd left it before camp, and yet nothing seemed the same. The macaroni was tasteless. She set it down on the coffee table.

"Call 203-555-3393," Mr. Crackers said.

"Quiet," Deena snapped.

"Call 203-555-3393," Mr. Crackers said, and there was something familiar about the way he said it that drew Deena's attention.

Deena frowned. She must be imagining things, but for a moment there Mr. Crackers had sounded a little like Alyssa. She walked over to his perch by the sofa. "Did you get that number from the television, or did someone teach you that?"

The bird regarded her solemnly. Smart as he was, he didn't speak English. Deena would have to try something else to get the answer. She coughed.

"P-U. Who cut the cheese?"

Okay. Not that prompt. She'd try another. "Call. . ."

"Call 203-555-3393." Mr. Crackers cocked his head just like he did when he expected a reward.

Again, she wasn't totally sure, but he sounded a lot like Alyssa. Deena gave the bird a bit of dried pineapple.

If Alyssa had taught the bird that number, it probably meant the number belonged to Spence. Should she call him?

Deena didn't think she had much to offer Spence. She couldn't cook, sew, iron, or do anything a good wife and mother should be able to do. And he might want more children. Did she really want to risk passing along any of her cancer genes? And yet hadn't she secretly always longed for children?

She closed her eyes. It was all too much to contemplate. Like standing atop that telephone pole and trying to take the Leap of Faith. She'd learned that wanting to put aside fears and actually being able to do it were two different things.

Yet looking back she wondered if she had missed the whole point of the exercise. Maybe it wasn't catching that trapeze bar that mattered. Maybe all God cared about was that she had taken a step in faith.

She thought about what had happened the night of the scavenger hunt. She could choose to believe Alyssa's asthma attack had been nothing more than an anxiety attack, or she could choose to believe something else had been at work— that God's voice had been whispering in her ear and telling her what to do.

If she believed this, then it was not too big a stretch to believe other things. That her mother's death had a purpose. It had served to direct her into research and had prompted her to reach out to women battling this disease as if they were her sisters.

It felt awkward, but thankfully no one saw her drop down on her knees and clasp her hands together.

I've been so angry at You for letting my mother get sick and die. Please forgive me for not trusting You, for turning away and thinking I could run my life better than You. Thank You for showing me the truth—for hearing me when I called out to You. I know I need to change. I want Your will for me.

The same commercial came on with the lawyer telling

viewers to call a toll-free number.

"Call 203-555-3393," Mr. Crackers said.

Deena closed her eyes tightly. She wanted a voice to assure her that she, Spence, and Alyssa could lead a long and happy life together. That she would stay cancer free and be able to balance a personal and professional life.

It didn't happen. There wasn't any lightning flash of insight into her life. But she became aware, gradually, of a peaceful feeling. As if just by bringing the problem to God, she'd found the answer.

She wasn't sure, but she thought it meant He was giving her a choice. She could call Spence or not—God would love her either way. If she chose to focus on her work, He would help her deal with the loneliness. If she called Spence, He would be there to rejoice or to console her if things didn't work out.

She could mess up or succeed, and God would love her just as much. No problem was bigger than Him, and there was nothing He could not overcome.

She rose. The phone sat on the kitchen counter. She stared at the black receiver. All she had to do was punch in the numbers Mr. Crackers had recited and she'd be talking to Spence. She picked up the receiver and set it down again.

She couldn't do it. She couldn't stand it if he was polite but distant, and she didn't know what she'd say if he seemed happy to hear from her.

It was the Leap of Faith all over again. She was too scared to take the jump. *Small steps,* Deena reminded herself. Small steps made in the faith that God would direct them.

One little phone call. She'd simply ask Spence how he and Alyssa were doing. She'd read some promising articles about new treatments in asthma. They could discuss that.

Before she changed her mind, she punched in the numbers.

A man answered on the first ring. "Joe's Pizza."

Deena very nearly dropped the phone. "I'm sorry. I must have the wrong number."

All this agony of wondering whether or not to call and what

to say. Stupid. Stupid. Stupid. Mr. Crackers had memorized a pizza parlor's phone number.

"Deena, please don't hang up."

It was Spence's voice, but what was he doing working in a pizza parlor? Deena discovered she didn't care. "Spence?"

"Yeah."

She gripped the phone harder. "How are you?"

"I'm fine," he said. "But your pizza is getting cold."

"I didn't order a pizza."

"And I don't work at Joe's," Spence said. "But I am standing downstairs, and I do have a pizza. Can I come up?"

She buzzed him up, and a moment later, there he was, all six feet four inches of him, standing at her front door with a pizza box. She pulled the door open wider, and he stepped inside.

"How did you know I was going to call you?" Deena asked.

"Call 203-555-3393," Mr. Crackers said.

Spence's gaze jerked to the bird, who watched them from his perch near the sofa. "What?"

"Every time someone says 'call,' he says your number."

"He sounds like Alyssa."

"I think she helped teach him your number." She gestured helplessly.

"I'm really glad she did, but I was coming here anyway to talk to you."

She stared at him, looking oddly just right in her condo. Pottery Barn meets mountain man. Would they both live happily ever after?

She folded her arms. "What did you want to talk about?"

He looked around for a place to set down the pizza box. Deena motioned him to the galley-style kitchen. He set the box on the counter. "I just didn't like the way we left things."

He looked so handsome and serious. That short, pale hair. His tan, rugged face. Those forest green eyes watching her so carefully. "I've been thinking a lot. And praying about this." He took a step toward her. "I don't know what the future holds for us, but I know the present isn't quite right without you."

Deena leaned against the refrigerator. The world was tilting just the way she'd wanted it, but it scared her so badly she didn't know what to do. "I. . .I could get cancer."

"And so could I. We're all in God's hands."

"Well, I can't cook."

"I don't want a cook. I want you. I want to get to know you better."

She shifted, and a magnet holding a takeout menu crashed to the ground. She couldn't take her gaze off him. "I don't know."

"That's okay. I do." He touched her cheek gently. His fingers were warm and wonderfully rough against her skin. "Deena, I love you. Will you give us a chance?"

The old fears were there pumping away beneath her skin with every beat of her heart. But there was faith as well, urging her to step forward, to love and let herself be loved.

God, I'm letting go.

"I say yes—a thousand times, yes." Deena placed her arms around his neck and lifted her face to his. He laughed and locked his arms around her. For a person who didn't like being hugged or hugging, she had to admit it felt pretty good.

He said her name softly, lovingly.

Deena tilted her head back to see his eyes. "Whoever thought I'd fall for the pizza delivery man?"

"The same person who knew I'd end up with Wonder Woman."

"I guess God is smiling pretty big right now," Deena said.

"Yeah. I think He is."

They looked at each other for a long moment, knowing what was to come and not wanting to hurry it. Finally, he tilted his head toward her.

Deena closed her eyes and fell into his kiss.

epilogue

six years later

"Can you believe it? We're going to be counselors this year!" Evie's voice, high and excited, overflowed into the hallway.

"You think one of us will get our old cabin?"

The stack of clothing nearly overflowed the plastic laundry basket as Deena stepped into Alyssa's bedroom. She set the basket on the bed and regarded both girls.

"Maybe," Deena said. "But whatever cabin you end up in, it'll be the right one. You'll see."

Alyssa, who had long given up her thick, black-rimmed glasses in favor of contact lenses, smiled up at her. "Did I tell you that Lourdes is going to be a counselor, too?"

"Only like a million times." Deena perched on the edge of the bed. During the past six years, both girls had changed so much.

Evie had grown to her full height—six feet—a full two inches taller than Deena herself. She would attend UConn in the fall and study child psychology. Alyssa, also bound for UConn, intended to go premed. Not into research, she'd explained almost apologetically, but into cardiology like her grandfather.

"So what are you going to do, Mom, with an empty house for a week?" Alyssa asked.

No matter how many times Deena heard that word, it still had the power to take her breath away. She'd never thought she'd marry, much less be a mother, yet she had been both these things for the past four years.

"The house won't be so empty," Deena teased. "Not with Spence and all the animals."

167

During the years, stray animals had a way of finding their way to the Rossi home. There was Mr. Crackers, a middle-aged bird now, close to thirty. Spence's German shepherd, Tyler, had passed away, but Spence had been unable to resist the pleading looks on the faces of two shaggy dogs he'd found by the side of the road one night. Several years ago Grandma Dixie had sent Alyssa a four-legged birthday present for her fourteenth birthday—a quirky but sweet thoroughbred named Willis who had been named after the Texas town where Grandma lived.

"I remember all the pranks I pulled that year you were our cabin counselor." Evie plucked at the bedspread. "I don't know how you put up with me."

"Oh, honey, that was the best week of my life. I wouldn't change one thing about it." Deena thought about the night Evie had unleashed the frogs and the morning she'd awakened to find herself wrapped in toilet paper.

"Remember how you couldn't hit our target in archery until we had you aim at the target to the right of ours?" Evie laughed. "Spence looked so surprised."

"And how you taught us to hula by downloading the instructions off the Internet?" Alyssa shook her head, sending her long blond ponytail flying. "That was so funny."

The three of them sat there together remembering. Of course for Deena, finding her faith and making a commitment to the Lord had been the pivotal moment of her life. Everything good that had happened to her could be traced back to the moment when she got down on her knees and gave her life to God.

So much had happened since then. She and Spence had started dating. The following summer when they'd returned to Camp Bald Eagle, he'd proposed to her during a moonlit walk on the dock. He'd gotten down on one knee and looked up at her with his heart in his eyes. "I love you," he'd said, "and I want to spend the rest of my life with you. Will you marry me?"

They'd gotten married on that dock, too. A summer wedding, of course, held right after the first camp session.

She'd worn her mother's wedding dress, and Stacy had cried when she'd seen Deena in it. "You look so beautiful," she'd said. "Mom and Dad would have been so happy."

"You look gorgeous, too," Deena said, handing her sister a tissue. Stacy wore a lilac-colored dress. She'd lost all her pregnancy weight and once again hardly weighed more than a hundred pounds.

"The music is about to start," Jeff said. "We should line up." He fingered the paper in his hands—a poem he had written just for this day. Deena hadn't heard it yet, but Stacy said it was beautiful.

Deena gripped her bouquet of flowers more tightly. A small crowd of well-wishers stood near the dock. She recognized Lourdes, Taylor, and Britty, who had come with family members. There were Quing and Andres and two more of her friends from the lab. Even Alyssa's grandparents had flown up from Texas to be there.

Deena's heart began to pound, and despite herself a flood of old doubts rushed through her mind. Could she really do this? *Absolutely,* her heart said. She wanted to do this.

Guitar music started, and Jeff walked Stacy down the pier. Alyssa, escorted by Deena's nephew Jack, went next. Evie followed, holding on to two-year-old Thomas's hand. The little boy scattered rose petals over the wooden planks. It was Deena's turn. The hem of her dress brushed the surface as she moved, every step bringing her closer to Spence and to a future she had never expected she would have. The light sparkling off the water was brighter than diamonds, and the blue sky was a joyous color. Her heart beat much too fast, not out of fear, but out of love for the man waiting for her at the end of the pier. Spence, tall and handsome in the navy suit. Spence, looking at her with so much love. Spence, the man with whom she would spend the rest of her life.

"Aunt Deena?"

Deena jerked back to the present. She had so much to be thankful for. She looked from Alyssa's face to Evie's. "Yes?"

"You okay?"

"Oh yeah, I'm just going to miss you all."

So soon they would be going off to college, leaving to begin their lives as adults. But what a blessing they had been to her. Sometimes she almost couldn't believe she was forty-one and cancer free.

She'd had some scares, but every six months she continued to get good reports. Each time it surprised her to hear someone actually say she was fine. Spence, however, firmly felt it was just not her time yet. Daily he encouraged and supported her research.

Sometimes Deena felt like pinching herself. She looked at Spence and couldn't believe that any two people could be so happy together. Oh, they had their fights—she still didn't like that motorcycle he'd bought—but mostly they were happy.

Maybe it was because they knew life could be fragile and had to be appreciated each and every day. But mostly, Deena thought, it was because of God's goodness. By His grace, she lived a life fuller than she ever could have imagined.

Sometimes she still dreamed of her mother. Not as she was, but how she could have been. In her dreams, her mother's face was unlined, smiling, and pain free. Her long black hair tumbled in a thick, wavy mass to her shoulders, just as Deena's did now. The face was her mother's, and it was also her own. It didn't matter that this was impossible. All Deena knew was they both were happy.

A Letter To Our Readers

Dear Reader:

In order that we might better contribute to your reading enjoyment, we would appreciate your taking a few minutes to respond to the following questions. We welcome your comments and read each form and letter we receive. When completed, please return to the following:

Fiction Editor
Heartsong Presents
PO Box 719
Uhrichsville, Ohio 44683

1. Did you enjoy reading *Leap of Faith* by Kim O'Brien?
   ❏ Very much! I would like to see more books by this author!
   ❏ Moderately. I would have enjoyed it more if

   _____

   _____

   _____

2. Are you a member of **Heartsong Presents**? ❏ Yes ❏ No
   If no, where did you purchase this book? _____

   _____

3. How would you rate, on a scale from 1 (poor) to 5 (superior), the cover design? _____

4. On a scale from 1 (poor) to 10 (superior), please rate the following elements.

   ____ Heroine   ____ Plot
   ____ Hero   ____ Inspirational theme
   ____ Setting   ____ Secondary characters

5. These characters were special because? _____
_____
_____

6. How has this book inspired your life? _____
_____
_____

7. What settings would you like to see covered in future
   Heartsong Presents books? _____
   _____
   _____

8. What are some inspirational themes you would like to see
   treated in future books? _____
   _____
   _____

9. Would you be interested in reading other **Heartsong
   Presents** titles? ❏ Yes ❏ No

10. Please check your age range:
    ❏ Under 18   ❏ 18-24
    ❏ 25-34   ❏ 35-45
    ❏ 46-55   ❏ Over 55

Name _____
Occupation _____
Address _____
City, State, Zip_____

Presents